John Pope-Hennessy

Sir Walter Raleigh in Ireland

John Pope-Hennessy

Sir Walter Raleigh in Ireland

ISBN/EAN: 9783337392154

Printed in Europe, USA, Canada, Australia, Japan

Cover: Foto ©Andreas Hilbeck / pixelio.de

More available books at **www.hansebooks.com**

SIR WALTER RALEGH
IN IRELAND

BY

SIR JOHN POPE HENNESSY

" To see that buried dust of living fame "

LONDON

KEGAN PAUL, TRENCH, & CO

MDCCCLXXXIII

CONTENTS

LETTERS OF SIR WALTER RALEGH FROM IRELAND, OR RELATING TO IRISH AFFAIRS

APPENDIX

SIR WALTER RALEGH IN IRELAND

Sir Walter's Study and the Geraldine College

A FEW years ago a desultory correspondent wrote
to a friend :—

"I have returned from the tropical seas where
Ralegh's fleet suffered from tornados and fever, and
I am resting for a few weeks in ' Sir Walter's study '
—in the same room where he looked at the charts
of Verazzano before his voyage, and where he first
smoked tobacco in Europe on his return. The
room is much the same as it might have been in
those times. The original painting of the first
governor of Virginia is there, and a contemporary

B   engraving

engraving of Elizabeth Queen of Virginia. The
long table at which he wrote, the oak chest in which
he kept papers, the little Italian cabinet, the dark
wainscoting with fine carvings rising up from each
side of the hearthstone to the ceiling, the old deeds
and parchments, some with Ralegh's seal, the
original warrant, under the autograph and signet
of Queen Elizabeth, granting a pension to the
Countess Elinor of Desmond, and the two book-
cases of vellum-bound and oak-bound books of the
fifteenth and sixteenth centuries—for there is
nothing in the room (except the writer of these
lines) that was not born when Ralegh lived here—
all these things compel me to think of him, and I
do my best to think well of him, but how can I?
Who could think well of him here? As I look
through the deep window where he often stood, I
see the ruined tower of St. Mary's and the remains
of the College of Youghal. They were built a
hundred years before his time, as well as the
warden's house in which he lived, by the eighth Earl
of Desmond. In this spot I cannot think of
Ralegh

Ralegh without thinking of Thomas Fitzgerald—a contrast not favourable to Ralegh."

The great Earl, to whom the modern occupant of Sir Walter's study thus referred, was the chief personage in the Pale for some years. He was Lord Deputy, but whilst he did his duty conscientiously to the foreign lord of Ireland, he was not insensible to the fact that there were people in Ireland who lived beyond the Pale. He called the first Parliament in which a real effort was made to establish something like fair dealing with the Irishry. He encouraged the commerce with the southern parts of Europe which had sprung up about the time that Edward the Second had farmed out the customs revenue of Cork, Youghal, and Waterford to Gerardo, a Florentine merchant, and the Friscobaldi had begun to send their wines from Livorno to Youghal. Like his contemporary Lorenzo de' Medici, he played a part in the revival of letters. He could not restore all the ruined seats of learning from Armagh to Cashel and Lismore that had fallen before civil war and foreign

B 2 invasion,

invasion, but he founded a college at Youghal in
1464 and gave the warden and fellows an endowment of £600 per annum—a more generous
endowment, looking to his income and the value of
money in those days, than the Parliament has given
to the Queen's Colleges and the Irish people themselves have given to the Catholic University in our
time.   Some of the specimens of early printing—
1479 to 1483—which were found fifty years ago in
a recess in the house built by the great Earl for the
Warden of the College, were no doubt a part of the
library then collected.   The contrast between this
generous effort to revive the ancient civilisation of
the country and the Philistine policy, as Mr.
Matthew Arnold would call it, of later times is
remarkable.

Ralegh and the Historians

Ralegh's career in Ireland determined his fate more perhaps than is usually supposed. On the other hand, his proceedings and those of his companions in Munster made a deep mark in Irish history. In fact he was one of the most daring and active of those eminent Englishmen who have done much to render British government permanently difficult—if not more than difficult—in Ireland.

British historians have touched but slightly on Ralegh's Irish exploits. Beyond the fact of his planting the potato for the first time in his garden near the old town-wall of Youghal, his smoking tobacco under the four intertwisted yew-trees that still remain there, and his musings with Edmund Spenser, little is published of his Munster life. And

yet

yet it is still a fresh and living force in the unwritten
history of the peasants from Youghal to Lismore,
and along the banks of the Blackwater and the Lee
from Imokilly to the mountains of Kerry.   It is
possible to meet men and women on the old
ploughlands of the Desmond estate who speak
nothing but Irish (in the Province of Munster there
are thirty thousand peasants who at this day do not
speak English), and from their stories to pick up
more of the real doings of Ralegh and his comrades
in Ireland than from Hume and the historians.
That tradition-loving and long-memoried people as
M. Thierry calls them, the most unchanging people
on the face of the globe as Mr. Froude calls them,
are not ignorant of the events of three hundred
years ago, and they look upon them now much
in the same way that their ancestors looked upon
them then.

In his ' English in Ireland' Mr. Froude makes no
reference to Sir Walter Ralegh, and in his ' History
of England from the Fall of Wolsey to the Death
of Elizabeth,' in which the war of the Desmonds

is

is more fully described, he hardly mentions him.
Having touched on the Irish victory at Glenmalure
in which the new Deputy, Lord Grey de Wilton,
was defeated, the landing of two thousand Scots in
Antrim under the Countess of Desmond, and the
landing of some Spanish and Italian allies of the
Irish in Dingle Bay, Mr. Froude says :—

" Meanwhile, Lord Grey having recovered as
well as he could from his first calamity, and being
reassured by a victory of Maltby's over the Burkes
and the unexpected quiet of the rest of Ireland,
gathered all the soldiers that he could raise, and set
off with a small, but, from its composition, un-
usually interesting force, to attack the invaders by
land. Ireland had become to young Englishmen
of spirit a land of hope and adventure, where they
might win glory and perhaps fortune ; and among
the names of the officers who accompanied Grey
are found those of Burghley's kinsman, young Mr.
Cheke, of Edmund Spenser, and of Walter Ralegh."

Such is Mr. Froude's mention of him. This
omission is not less remarkable from the fact that in
important

important events described by Mr. Froude, Ralegh took a busy part ; and for a score of years he was an influential adviser of Elizabeth, sometimes the most influential, in an Irish policy that, as Edmund Burke says, was never deviated from for a single hour during her reign.

III

Arrives in Ireland

Spenser was Assistant-Secretary to the Lord Deputy, and was then twenty-eight years of age. Ralegh was also in his twenty-eighth year when he sailed from the Isle of Wight for Ireland.   He landed in Cove harbour with what he calls "a footeband of one hundrethe men."   In his letter to Lord Burghley written from Cork on the 22nd of February, 1580, he claims certain arrears, from which it seems that he was paid at the rate of four shillings a day for himself, two shillings a day for

his

his lieutenant, fourteenpence a day for four other officers, and eightpence a day for every common soldier. To this company he was able to add a small number of horsemen with "good furniture," that is, suitable armour and trappings. They were mostly Devonshire men, and, like their captain. full of courage and energy. Even when, two years later, by the Queen's special order, he got the command of Captain Appesley's band also, the number of troops with which he operated was very small. The amount of destruction and conquest accomplished by those highly paid and well equipped men seems out of all proportion to their insignificant numbers. For some years the Irish fell before them as German tribes had fallen before the soldiers of Italy.

IV

• The Slaughter at Smerwick

Captain Ralegh's "Reckonings" in Ireland
begin, according to the records in the Rolls Office,
with the date July 13, 1580, a couple of months
before Lord Grey's second government in Ireland,
but some earlier record of his pay may have been
lost. Whether or not he preceded the Lord
Deputy to Ireland, he certainly accompanied him
to the bay on the shores of the Atlantic where
Admiral Winter and Vice-Admiral Bingham
blockaded Desmond's six or seven hundred foreign
allies. Hemmed in on all sides, the garrison of
Smerwick Castle surrendered on the 10th of
November, 1580. Here is Mr. Froude's description
of the way in which some of those young Englishmen of spirit began to win glory :—

"Don Bastian with the officers came out with
ensigns

ensigns trailing, and gave themselves up as prisoners. The men piled their arms outside the walls, and waited defenceless to learn the pleasure of their conquerors. They were strangers, and by this time alone. The officers were reserved for their ransom. Common prisoners were inconvenient and expensive, and it was thought desirable to read a severe lesson to Catholic sympathisers in Ireland. 'The Lord of hosts,' wrote Grey, 'had delivered the enemy to us, none of ours being hurt, Mr. Cheke alone excepted. Then put I in certain bands, who fell straight to execution.' A certain number of the original party had fallen sick, and had been sent back to Spain. With the exception of these and of the officers, the entire party was slaughtered. A few women, some of them pregnant, were hanged. A servant of Saunders, an Irish gentleman, and a priest were hanged also. The bodies, six hundred in all, were stripped and laid out upon the sands, 'as gallant goodly personages,' said Grey, 'as ever were beheld.'"

Mr. Froude, after referring to Camden's statement

ment that Lord Grey had shed tears and Queen
Elizabeth had wished the cruelty undone, surmises
that they might possibly " have felt some pity for
the subjects of the King of Spain which was refused
to the wives and babies of the Irish chiefs." But
he gives good reasons for doubting Lord Grey's
tears or the sincerity of the Queen's pity.

Whoever was to blame for the occurrence, the
English admiral had no complicity in it. Dr.
Taylor in his ' History of Ireland ' says : " To the
relentless soldiery innocence furnished no protection ; helpless infancy and tottering age found no
mercy. Admiral Winter, however, with the human-
ity natural to a British sailor, was shocked by the
horrid massacre, and granted protection to a few
that escaped to his fleet." But who was to blame ?
Lord Grey does not say what orders he gave to the
bands he sent in, nor who commanded them. He
does not mention Ralegh's name in his despatch of
November 12 to the Privy Council. The question
as to who was the actual executioner seems, however, to be set at rest by a passage in the contemporary

porary narrative in Hooker's Supplement to the Chronicles of Holinshed, in which we are told that the people in the fort held out a white flag, uttering the cry, "Misericordia, misericordia;" they then, at the Lord Deputy's request, disarmed themselves, all their armour and arms being laid in one place. Hooker then adds: "In the fort Sir James Fitzgerald, Knight, and Lord of the Decies, was a prisoner by the order of the Earl of Desmond; and one Plunket, an Irishman, and one Englishman which came and accompanied the traitors out of Spaine. The knight was set at liberty, but the other two were executed. When the captain had yielded himself, and the fort appointed to be surrendered, Captain Ralegh, together with Captain Macworth, who had the ward of that day, entered into the castle, and made a great slaughter, many or most part of them being put to the sword." The exact number thus dealt with by Ralegh and Macworth, though not given in Hooker's Supplement, appears in Holinshed under the date An. Reg. 23 (1580). "The fort was yeelded, all the Irish men and women

women hanged; and more than foure hundred
Spaniards, Italians, and Biscaies put to the sword;
the coronell, capteins, secretarie and others, to the
number of twentie, saved for ransome."

V

Elizabeth's Approval

Mr. Froude is the first English historian who
admits that Queen Elizabeth had sanctioned this
early exploit of Grey and Ralegh.   For nearly three
centuries the royal approbation of the Mahometan
lesson of Smerwick was denied or doubted by
British writers, whilst on the other hand the popular
belief in Ireland was universal, that Grey had
broken faith and that Elizabeth had approved of
the massacre.   Lord Bacon said, "The Queen was
much displeased at the slaughter."*   Leland em-
bodied the general view of the historians from

* 'Harleian MSS.,' vol. v. p. 89.

Camden

Camden to the nineteenth century when he said, "Queen Elizabeth expressed the utmost concern and displeasure at this barbarous execution, but such pretences and such professions could not efface the odiousness of this action, and on the Continent it was received with horror." The two letters, however, from Elizabeth to the Lord Deputy, printed in the appendix, show that the popular Irish view was well founded. The first letter is dated December 12, 1580, and is in reply to Lord Grey's despatch of the 12th of November. In this letter she says the deed performed by him was " greately to our lyking." The second letter was written by the Queen two years subsequently, and refers with satisfaction to his exploit. They were both rendered accessible to the public only a few years ago when the State Papers were calendared at the Public Record Office.

The mistaken view of the British historians may possibly have arisen from assuming that because Lord Burghley had condemned the massacre, his Royal mistress had condemned it also. But this

was

was only one of many instances in which the English Prime Minister of that day differed with Elizabeth as well as with the Dublin Castle officials. What real ground the Irish people have for the proverb, " The faith of Grey," as indicating a broken promise, is difficult to determine. Grey's despatches give no colour to any act of treachery. His secretary Edmund Spenser, however, admits the existence of a vague sentiment on the subject, from which he defends his master. But as regards the approval of the Queen, which is now beyond all question, the accuracy of the popular view in Ireland as opposed to that of the historians, may be accounted for by the fact that whilst Lord Burghley spoke out in London against the massacre, and the Queen held her tongue, Lord Grey, doubtless, showed her letters to his Council, and perhaps to the captains who were most zealous at Smerwick. It is one of the misfortunes of foreigners under such circumstances that the gossip of the dinner-table and the camp is soon spread by native servants.

The

The State Papers that can now be read by the public at the Rolls Office, determine another disputed point also in connection with this affair. The Abbé Mac Geoghegan had asserted that one or two of the prisoners had been tortured and mutilated before being put to death. This was denied as a malicious fable. It was asserted that though Elizabeth's gallant captains might deal out stern justice to Irish women and children, to the extent even of hanging them, they would not wantonly mutilate human beings. One of the official reports however to Sir Francis Walsingham, the Queen's Secretary of State, in the seventy-eighth volume of the State Papers relating to Ireland for 1580, makes the following mention of the torture and mutilation :—

" The ffortes were yielded, all the Irishmen and women hanged, and four hundred and upwardes of Italyans and others put to the sworde. . . . A ffrayer and others kept in store to be executed after examination had of them. . . . Next day was executed an Englishman who served Dr. Saunders,

C   one

one Plunckett, and an Irishe Priest theire armes
and legges were broken and hanged upon a
gallows."

VI

Ralegh's Courage

Some of Ralegh's exploits were such as would
entitle him now-a-days to the Victoria Cross.   In his
letter from Cork to Sir Francis Walsingham, of
February 23, 1581, after he had been about a year
in Ireland, he refers to an escape he had from the
Seneschal of Imokilly when returning by a circuitous
route from Dublin to Cork.   His own account of
the skirmish, which seems to have taken place at the
Ballinacurra river, is very modest :—

"In my return from Develin I made a hard
escape from the Seneshall in Barre's countre (wher
he is always fostered) with xiiii horsmen and threescore footmen.

"I was three horsmen, and soun set on horsbacke

two

two Irishe footmen. I coveted to recover a litle old castle, in that resun I left three men and three horses. The manner of myne own behaviour I leve to the report of others, but the escape was strange to all men. The castle was a longe mile off from the place wher he first sett on us. Ther is great need of a supply in Munster, for the bandes are all miche decayed."

From that letter Walsingham would learn nothing of the fact that Ralegh most gallantly risked his own life to save one of his followers. Hooker's description of the affair is more minute :—

"The capteine (Ralegh) making his returne from Dubline, and the same well knowne unto the seneschall of Imokellie, through whose countrie he was to passe, laie in ambush for him to haue intrapped him betweene Youghall and Corke, lieng at a foord, which the said capteine must passe our with six horssemen, and certain kerne. The capteine little mistrusting anie such matter, had in his companie onelie two horssemen and foure shot on horssebacke, which was too small a force in so

C 2   doubtfull

doubtfull and dangerous times : neuertheless he had a very good guide, which was the servant of John Fitzedmunds of Cloue, a good subject, and this guide knew euerie corner and starting hole in those places.

" The capteine being come towards the foord, the seneschal had spied him alone, his companie being scattered behind, and verie fiercelie pursued him, and crossed him as he was to ride ouer water, but yet he recovered the foord and was passed ouer. The Irishman who was his guide, when he saw the capteine thus alone, and so narrowlie distressed, he shifted for himselfe and fled into a broken castell fast by, there to saue himselfe. The capteine being thus ouer the water, Henrie Moile, riding alone about a bowes shoot before the rest of his companie, when he was in the midle of the foord his horsse foundred and cast him downe ; and being afraid that the seneschalls men would have folowed him and have killed him, cried out to the capteine to come and to save his life ; who not respecting the danger he himselfe was in, came unto him, and recovered

covered both him and his horsse. And then Moile wishing with all haste to leape up, did it with such hast and vehemencie that he quite over lept the horsse and fell into a mire fast by, and so his horsse ran awaie and was taken by the enemie. The capteine neverthelesse staid still, and did abide for the coming of the residue of his companie, of the foure shot which as yet were not come foorth, and for his man Jenkin who had about two hundred pounds in monie about him, and sat upon his horsse in the mean while, having his staffe in one hand, and his pistoll charged in the other hand."

The chronicler adds that the Seneschal, though he was twenty to one in strength, would not face Ralegh's little band again when he saw the captain ready to receive the onset. A leader who risked his life for his soldiers was likely to be well served by them, and when in another skirmish with the Irish his horse was mortally wounded by a dart, Ralegh was saved by two of his band fighting for him against long odds. Hooker gives a vivid account of this :—

*   " When

"When the summer was spent, Captaine Ralegh returned with all his band unto Corke, being in number eight horssemen and four score footmen. And as he passed through the countrie, it was advertised to him that David Barrie, an archtraitor, was at Clone with a great troope of sundrie hundreds of men. Whereupon he thought good to passe that waie through the towne of Clone, minding to trie the valor of David Barrie, if by anie meanes he might meet with him. And euen at the verie towns end he found Barrie and all his companie, and with a lustie courage gave the onset upon him. But Barrie refused it, and fled. And then this capteine passing from thense, in his jorneie he espied in a plaine niere adjoining to a woods sides a companie of footmen by themselves, upon whome with six horssemen he gave the charge; but these being cut off from the wood whereunto they were flieng, and having not succor now to helpe and relieve themselves, they turned backe and conjoining themselves together to withstand this force and onset made upon them, in which they behaved

behaved themselves verie valiantlie, and of the
horsses they killed five, of which Capteine Ralegh
his horsse was one, and he himselfe in great danger,
and like to have beene slaine, if his trustie servant
Nicholas Wright a Yorkshire man borne had not
bin. For he perceiving that his maisters horsse
was galled and stricken with a dart, and plunged so
much, that to his seeming he was past service, the
said Nicholas willed and called to an Irishman
there, whose name was Patrike Fagaw, that he
should looke to his capteine, and either to rescue
him, or to give charge upon the enemie. Whereupon the said Fagaw rescued his capteine, and the
said Nicholas Wright forthwith gave the onset upon
six of the enemies and slue one of them. And
therewith came one James Fitzrichard an Irish
gentlemen with his kerne to the rescue of the
capteine, but his kerne was slaine and himselfe in
danger. For Wright not looking on them followed
the enemie verie egerlie and recompensed the losse
of one with the slaughter of others. Which
Capteine Ralegh perceiving cried out to his man
saieng,

saieng, 'Wright, if thou be a man, charge above
hand and save the gentleman.' Who at his
maisters commandment pressed into the middle of
the enemies, and slue one of them and so saved the
gentleman : and in which skirmish his horsse leg
was cut under him.   Diverse footmen were slaine
of the enemies, and two were taken prisoners,
whome they carried with them to Corke."

His arrest of Lord and Lady Roche about this
time has been described as a gallant exploit; but
though it involved some danger it was not done
without an act of treachery on Ralegh's part, and
an abuse of hospitality.

Some of the details of the exploit, as given in
Hooker's Chronicles, are characteristic.   Zouch
having directed him to capture Lord Roche,
Ralegh ordered ninety of his band "to be in
readyness between ten and eleven o'clock at night
upon the paine of death ;" and at the appointed
hour, on a dark night, he marched out of the north
gate of Cork, and for twenty miles through an
enemy's country.   At daybreak he reached Lord
Roche's

Roche's castle. The villagers adjoining the castle assembled to the number of five hundred, armed with darts and spears. Ralegh placed his well-equipped men across the village, and with six, whose names are given, Butler, Fulford, Wright, Barlow, Swane, and Pinking Huish, he knocked at the gate. A parley ensued, Ralegh stating that he came to speak to his lordship. After some discussion it was proposed that he should be allowed to pass in, provided he would only bring with him two or three of his party. To this Ralegh agreed, and the gate was then opened. "When once within the gate," says the chronicler, "Captain Ralegh so handled the matter by devises and meanes, that by little and little, and by some and some, he had gotten in within the iron doore or gate of the courlodge all his men." He then directed that every man should have "his peece well prepared with two bullets."

Lord Roche received him with great courtesy, presented him to his lady and invited him to join them in the meal they were about taking. Ralegh accepted

accepted the hospitality, and then asked Lord and Lady Roche to accompany him back to Cork. His lordship declined the invitation, whereupon Ralegh pointed out that his armed soldiers commanded the hall where they sat, that Lord Roche was his prisoner, and that he and his lady would be compelled to accompany him. With Lord Roche's life in his hands, he had no difficulty in getting orders given to the villagers to make no opposition to the departure from the castle. The return journey was begun at midnight, amidst a storm of rain. The darkness and the tempest saved him from an attack by the Seneschal of Imokilly, who lay with eight hundred men close to the main road. His contemporary historian describes the path he took as being "full of balks, hillocks, pits and rocks." Some of his men were much hurt by stumbling in the dark and "some lost their armour." One soldier appears to have died of a hurt or from exhaustion. After his two night marches, he arrived at the walls of Cork, early in the morning, "to the great joy of the garrison."

In

In August 1580, Sir James Fitzgerald, the Earl
of Desmond's brother, was captured and brought
to Cork, where he was tried by Captain Ralegh
and Captain Sentleger. They sentenced him to be
hanged, drawn and quartered. Portions of his body
remained for a considerable time above the gates of
the city. The other brother, Sir John of Desmond,
was killed in the following year and his body
brought to Ralegh, who was acting as Governor
of Cork. His head was sent to Dublin Castle, and
his body was suspended by the heels from a high
gibbet over the river Lee, on the north-gate bridge
of Cork, where it swung for three years. Before
long the skeleton of the Earl was also hanging from
the walls of Cork, his head having been sent as " a
goodly gift to Her Highnesse " in London. "Such
was the fate," says the Abbé MacGeoghegan, " of the
illustrious Fitzgeralds of Desmond, the Maccabees
of our day, who sacrificed their lives and properties
in the defence of the Catholic cause." For eight
and twenty years from this time, Ralegh's name
is found associated with the broken fortunes of the
Geraldines

Geraldines until the burial of James, the Eighteenth
Earl, in the Chapel of the Tower.

VII

His Hardships

The longer he served, however, the more he
complained of the hardships he and his soldiers
endured. In a letter dated in 1581, " From Corke,
the fyrst of May," he thus writes to the Lord
Deputy of Ireland, Lord Grey de Wilton :—

"The bandes of Sir Georg Bowser, Edward
Barkley, Captayne Dowdall, and of my self have
bine ever since the seconde weeke of Lent
remayning in Corke ; and both the great wood of
Conoloathe, Harlo, Clenlis, and all the countie of
Lymbricke, and the counties betweene the Dingle
and Kilkeny, left without any companies ether to
defend itself or anoy the enemy. Since which tyme
wee have made two journeys : the one towards
Kilkeny

Kilkeny to give convoye to my Lorde, and attend his returne, and the other into Conoloathe, by which jurnes (the one being in horible wether, and the other utterly botles, being don without draught or espiall, and beside inforst to walke such unreasonable marches as, wher wee dispatched a churell of the traitors, wee lamed, lost, or left behynde unserviceable, a soldier or two of our owne) the poore bands have curste the change they made in levying to follow your Honor, as they have tould the Lord Generall many tymes. And this fyrst of May wee ar going another posting convoy towards Kilkeny. But to culler the matter, wee shall march some two dayes out of our way to seeke wee know not whome. The store of Cork, except it be a smale quantitie of wheat and butter, is all spent within the walles, and now it wilbe aleged that wee cannot serve for want of vittles, or else because the bandes are not supplied ; although wee were nevere less than fore hundred stronge, and yet both of Sir George Bowcer's and Captain Barkle's companies left at Kilmalloch and Asketon. Wee

have

have spent these two monethes of the spring in
parles with Barrey Rowe, the Countess of
Desmond, and Finnin Macartey; and wee think
it willbe two moneth more er he (Ormond) be
resolved whether thes oughte to be followed or no,
and yet theris no day passeth without some
trayterous villanies by the Barres committed."

VIII

The Queen and Ralegh

Some evidence of the personal interest Elizabeth
began to take in Ralegh is manifest in the following
letter she sent to the Lord Deputy in April 1582.

By the Queene.

" Right trusty and wellbeloued.   We grete youe
well.   Where we be given to vnderstand that
Capteyne Appesley is not longe synce deceased,
and the band of footemen which he had, committed

nowe

nowe to James Fenton : for that as we are en-
fourmed the said fenton hathe otherwise an entreteynment by a certeyn ward vnder his charge ;
but chieflye for that our pleasure is to haue our
Servaunt Walter Rawley treyned some longer tyme
in that our realme for his better experience in
Martiall affaires, and for the speciall care we haue
to doe him good in respecte of his kyndred, that
haue served vs some of them (as you knowe) neer
aboute our Parson : theise are to requier youe, that
the leading of the said bande may be committed
to the said Rawley. And for that he is for so
manie considerations by vs—lycensed to staye here
and owre pleasure is that the said bande shall be in
the meane tyme (till he repaire into that realme)
deliuered to so manie sooche as he shall depot to
be his luietenant there. Given at our Mannor of
Grenewiche the   of Aprill 1582 in the xxiiij[th]
yere of our reigne."

Three years later she writes to Dublin that a
substitute is to be found for Rafe Lane, " in consideration

sideration of his undertaking the voyage to Virginia for Sir Water Rawley." In 1587, she refers to a fresh levy of horsemen for service in Ireland made by "our well beloved Sir Walter Rawley." In that year she places him first in the list of her Irish Captains. When she issues a sort of Royal Commission "touching the service in Ireland against Tyrone," Ralegh is one of the six selected to advise her. His growing influence with the Queen can be noted in his letters on Irish affairs.

IX

The Success of his Bands

A question of some historic interest is solved by a study of Ralegh's Irish campaigns, and indeed by his own admission. How can we account for the success of such small bodies of soldiers as Elizabeth's captains commanded in the Desmond wars? The bands of Piers, Appesley, and Ralegh seemed

seemed for some years to be invincible. Not counting the women and children who were deliberately and systematically butchered,* they routed over and over again five times their number of Irish gallowglasses ; indeed, if Hooker is to be believed, sometimes ten times their number. And yet in the lifetime of Ralegh this was all changed. He lived to hear of Hugh O'Neill, who, to use Mr. Froude's words, destroyed an English army at the ford of the Blackwater—the northern Blackwater. Something of course was due to the courage and skill of men like Ralegh, and the fatal rivalry of the Geraldines and Butlers. But such causes could not account for the early and easy victories over numerous Irish, compared with the fact that under Hugh O'Neill, Owen Roe, and the still later Sarsfield, the Irish troops were a match for an equal number of the enemy, and sometimes defeated the English troops even with a force numerically inferior to them. Ralegh himself

---

* Lecky, 'Eighteenth Century,' vol. ii. p. 105.

D   explained

explained it. In his 'Discourse touching a War with Spain,' one of his miscellaneous works not printed till after his death, he says :—

" I myself remember that, within these thirty years, two of her Majesty's ships would have commanded 100 sail of the Spaniards. I remember also, when I was a captain in Ireland, 100 foot and 100 horse would have beaten all the forces of the strongest province. But of late I have known an Easterling fight hand to hand with one of her Majesty's ships, and the Irish in this last war have been victorious with an equal or even with an inferior force. And what is the reason? The Netherlands in those days had wooden guns and the Irish had darts: but the one is now furnished with as great a number of English ordnance as ourselves, and the other with as good pikes and muskets as England hath."*

Thus Voltaire's libel, which had its origin in the contrast between such campaigns as Ralegh's in

* Ralegh's ' Miscellaneous Works,' vol. viii. pp. 304–5.

Ireland

Ireland and the subsequent achievements of the Irish brigade on the Continent, is answered by Ralegh himself.

X

Practises the Assassination of Irish Chiefs

But apart from the fact that for many years the Irish were not met with even weapons, for which of course no one can blame the soldiers, the captains of Elizabeth introduced an infamous system as new to Ireland in the days of Ralegh as the English muskets. In the fifth book of his 'History of the World' Ralegh discusses the difference between "killing a man in open field with even weapons, and killing by guile." Writing in the prison of the Tower, he condemns the "lying in wait for bloud privily," as "guilfull murder," yet there seems little doubt that he had previously encouraged, if not practised, the assassination of

D 2   the

the Irish landlords and chiefs of his time. He had
high official example to guide him. " Practice and
subornation," writes Secretary Fenton to Walsingham, "is as necessary as force." Instead of killing
the greatest landowner in Munster by what he calls
the "uncertain end of arms," the Chief Secretary
of that day records how he told the Lord President
to get some one to undertake that service " for the
hire of a thousand pounds, with some further small
gratification of Desmond's lands." The latest
biographer of Ralegh, Mr. Edward Edwards,
thus deals with his complicity in such trans-
actions :

"On one other important matter, Ralegh,
Carew, and Cecil were at one. In regard to what,
in the phrase of their day, were called 'practices
against rebels,' they were as little troubled with
scruples of conscience as Sir Humphrey Gilbert, or
Sir Henry Sidney, or Arthur Lord Grey of Wilton
had been a few years earlier. In plain English,
'practices against rebels' meant the deliberate
assassination of rebels, or even of persons
vehemently

vehemently suspected of an intention to rebel. Cecil indeed avowed that he had a rooted objection to the killing of a rebel by poison."

Mr. Edwards here refers to Cecil's objection to the proposal to get rid of the Earl of Tyrone by poison; but I doubt if it is fair to place him exactly on the same footing in this matter as Ralegh and Carew. The latter certainly thought any means lawful by which the lands of the Irish chiefs could be obtained. Mr. Froude quotes a letter of his, written in 1602 to the Lord Deputy Mountjoy, in which he describes how Hugh O'Donnell, who had gone to Spain for assistance, was followed by a hired assassin, who poisoned him in the castle of Simancas. The assassin, Carew writes, "at his coming in Spain was suspected by O'Donnell, because he embarked at Cork; but afterwards he insinuated his access and O'Donnell is dead. He never told the President in what manner he would kill him; but did assure him it should be effected." In Carew's original letter in the Public Record Office, he says, "O'Donnell is poisoned." The words

words "poisoned," "President," and "kill" are in cipher. That Ralegh and Cecil were not entirely of one mind on this subject seems probable from the following letter, written, Mr. Payne Collier thinks, when Ralegh was in Ireland in October 1598 :—

To the Right Honorable Sir Robert Cecil, Knight,
Principall Secretory to Her Majestie.

"Sir,—It can be no disgrace if it weare knowen that the killinge of a rebel weare practised ; for you see that the lives of anoynted princes are daylye sought, and we have always in Ireland geven head money for the killing of rebels who ar evermore proclaymed at a price. So was the Earle of Desmonde and so have all rebels been practised against. Notwithstanding I have written this enclosed to Stafford who only recommended that knave to me upon his credit. Butt for your sealf, you are not to be touched in the matter. And for

me

me, I am more sorrye for beinge deceaved than for being declared in the practise.

"Your Lordships ever to do you service,

"W. RALEGH.

"He hathe nothinge under my hand butt a passport."

The knave who got the passport was a paid murderer. Mr. Edwards surmises that the "being deceaved" refers to a case in which Sir George Carew describes how he himself had hired an assassin, to whom he gave "a pistoll, some munitions, and ten pounds in money," to kill John Fitz Thomas, the owner of a fine estate, but "one Coppinger, sometime a footman to Sir Walter Ralegh, who had promised him (the assassin) faythfullye to assist him," snatched the weapon from his hand as he was about to shoot Fitz-Thomas in Arlow Woods, where they were passing with him alone.

XI

Elizabeth's Complicity in Assassination Plots

Nor was it the example merely of the Deputies, Chief Secretaries, and the Presidents of Munster, with whom he associated in Ireland, that Ralegh had to guide him in this dark path. He had opportunities of knowing the Queen's secret sentiments, and he could hardly have been ignorant of the confidential precedents established by those who immediately preceded him in the career of "glory and fortune" in Ireland. The manuscripts calendared in our time by the Rolls Office terminate a controversy raised by John O'Neill, the great chief of Ulster, three hundred years ago. When Sir Henry Sidney invited him to an interview within the Pale, the answer was that "he had much affection for Sir Henry, but that the Deputy's predecessor, the Earl of Sussex, had twice attempted

attempted to assassinate him. That after such experience his timorous Irish would not trust him any more in English hands." Up to a recent period historians denounced this as a " foul libel upon the blunt and honest Sussex." The national traditions, however, had always supported O'Neill's charges. It was a question of the belief of the long-memoried people on the one side, and the incredulity of ill-informed writers on the other. But now the controversy is at an end. Mr. Froude himself has given the conclusive evidence to the world. In a letter from the Earl of Sussex to Queen Elizabeth, written from Ardbrachan on the 24th of August, 1561, he describes the arrival of two messengers from the camp of the victorious Irish chief, one of whom, named Grey, he proceeded to bribe.

" 'I swore him upon the Bible,' writes the Lord Deputy, 'to keep secret that I should say unto him, and assured him, if it were known during the time I had the government there, that besides the breach of his oath it should cost him his life. I used long circumstance in persuading him to serve your

your Highness, to benefit his country, and to procure assurance of living to him and his for ever by doing of that which he might easily do. He promised to do what I woud. In fine I brake with him to kill Shan O'Neill : and bound myself by an oath to see him have a hundred marks of land by the year to him and to his heirs for his reward. He seemed desirous to serve your Highness and to have the land : but fearful to do it, doubting his own escape after with safety, which he confessed and promised to do by any means he might escaping with his life.' "

Having quoted this despatch, Mr. Froude says : " Elizabeth's answer—if she sent any answer—is not discoverable. It is most sadly certain, however, that Sussex was continued in office." He adds : " The Lord Deputy's assassination plots were but the forlorn resources of a man who felt his work too heavy for him." Two years after this the English troops were again routed. A treaty of peace was accordingly made.

" Indentures were drawn " (says Mr. Froude) " on the

the 17th of December 1563, in which the Ulster sovereignty was transferred to O'Neill in everything but the name ; and a treaty—such treaty as it was —required only Elizabeth's signature. When a second dark effort was made to cut the knot of the Irish difficulty. As a first evidence of returning cordiality a present of wine was sent to Shan O'Neill from Dublin. It was consumed at his table, but the poison had been unskilfully prepared. It brought him and half his household to the edge of death, but no one actually died. The guilt could not be fixed on Sussex. The crime was traced to an English resident in Dublin named Smith ; and if Sussex had been the instigator, his instrument was too faithful to betray him."

But why should Smith betray the Lord Deputy ? When put upon his trial he " confessed his guilt, took the entire responsibility upon himself, and declared that his object was to rid his country of a dangerous enemy." Smith no doubt knew that, though weak in the field, the Lord Deputy had influence in Dublin, and the result was that the convicted

convicted poisoner got off without punishment. Mr. Froude thinks the treachery of the Lord Deputy, the conduct of the inquiry, and the anomalous termination of it, would have been incredible had not the original correspondence, in which the facts are not denied, been now before us. Referring to the Queen's answer to John O'Neill's remonstrance against being thus practised upon, Mr. Froude says: "After the repeated acts of treachery which had been at least meditated towards O'Neill with Elizabeth's knowledge, she was scarcely justified in assuming a tone of innocent anger."

Ralegh knew all this. He knew also that Sir Henry Sidney had finally succeeded where Sussex failed, and that he succeeded by employing a friend and companion of Ralegh. Dr. Taylor describes how the Irish chief proceeded to the camp of the Hebridean Scots. "But," he goes on to say, "an emissary of the Government had preceded him. Piers, a British officer, a disgrace to his country and his profession, had undertaken the task of

persuading

persuading the Scottish chief to murder his unsuspecting guest. At a given signal, the banqueting room was filled with soldiers, and all the Irish were slain. O'Neill's head was sent to Dublin, and Piers received a thousand marks from the Government as a reward for the murder." Hooker tells us that the head was carried to the Lord Deputy " by Captain Piers, by whose device the stratagem, or rather tragedie, was practised." Mr. Froude, whilst admitting that O'Neill and his friends in the banqueting hall were murdered, says but little of Captain Piers' conduct. " Four days later," he tells us, "Piers hacked the head from the body and carried it on a spear's point through Drogheda to Dublin, where, staked upon a pike, it bleached on the battlements of the castle, a symbol to the Irish world of the fate of Celtic heroes." But Mr. Froude, perhaps, sees that it was a symbol to the Irish world of something else too.

XII

Burghley disapproves of Oppression

This Captain Piers, Captain Ralegh, and Sir William Morgan were subsequently joined in the one commission under which they exercised martial law, or rather martial executions without law, in the county of Cork. The lessons which were thus taught to Ralegh, and which he practised without scruple, gained him a great estate and the confidence of Elizabeth, but did not serve him in certain other influential quarters. The Lord Treasurer did not like such work. He had contributed to the true glory of his own country and the future happiness of the Netherlands by denouncing the bloody Duke of Alva and opposing the bigotry and tyranny of the foreign rulers of Holland. He looked askance at Sir Walter Ralegh, and treated many of his importunities with silence

silence. The year after Ralegh had written from Cork complaining that the Earl of Ormond was not severe enough in Munster, and that what was wanted was the fire and sword of Sir Humphrey Gilbert (Ralegh's half-brother), who boasted of "putting man, woman, and child to death," Lord Burghley wrote to Sir Henry Wallop, the War Treasurer for Ireland, on the 10th of June, 1582, "that the Flemings had not such cause to rebel against the oppression of the Spaniards as the Irish against the tyranny of England." In repeating this sentence of the greatest statesman of the sixteenth century, Mr. Froude * observes with truth that Lord Burghley possessed the rare quality of being able to recognise the faults of his own countrymen.

---

* 'History of England,' x. vol. p. 604.

XIII

Burghley's Policy thwarted

But in spite of his commanding position, the English Minister failed. Not for the first or last time, the officials in Ireland thwarted and defeated the good intentions of a statesman in London. Lord Burghley touched the root of the evil, when he instructed the Treasurer Wallop, that confiscated lands in Ireland were not to be given to persons, but to offices.* Writing from Dublin, Sir Henry Wallop bitterly complains of these instructions, and of " the Lord High Treasurer's harshness " in the matter. It is evident that the Queen and Walsingham did not concur with the Prime Minister. Had the policy of the Prime Minister been carried out, the Devon and Dorset adven-

---

* ' State Papers '—Ireland, vol. xci. p. 2.

turers

turers would have returned to their homes in England, with whatever pay they might have saved, instead of remaining in Ireland as alien landlords. Lord Burghley's instructions would have enabled some lands to be attached to the office of Governor or Deputy Governor of Cork, but Sir Walter Ralegh would not have got the castles and farms and abbey lands along the shores of the Black-water. The English Minister of that day fore-saw what the English historian who describes the period has exposed, the effect upon the Irish people of rewarding the adventurers with land. "These western gentlemen," says Mr. Froude, "had been trained in the French wars, in the privateer fleets, or on the coast of Africa, and the lives of a few thousand savages were infinitely unimportant to them. The extinction of the Irish was contemplated with as much indifference as the destruction of the Red Indians by the politicians of Washington, and their titles to their lands as not more deserving of respect. The Irish, it is true, were not wholly savages ; they belonged, as much as the English

E   themselves

themselves, to the Arian race; they had a history, a literature, laws and traditions of their own, and a religion which gave half Europe an interest in their preservation; but it is no less certain that to these intending colonists they were of no more value than their own wolves, and would have been exterminated with equal in-difference."*

Ralegh has been censured for recommending his half-brother's vigorous measures, but in justice to him it should be remembered that his most inti-mate companions have recorded similar deeds of their own when claiming Irish lands or seeking preferment. Sir Nicholas Malbie, writing to Wal-singham in April 1580, says:—

" This day the forces which I have entertained took the strong castle of Dwnemene from Shane MacHubert and put the ward, both men, women, and children to the sword." Captain Zouche, at the same time, reports to the Secretary of State

* ' History of England,' vol. x. ch. 59, p. 233.

the

the taking of a castle in the county of Limerick in these words :—

"They made no defence of fyght, butt the howse being entered they yielded, and sum sought to swim away, but there escaped nott one, neither of man, woman, nor child." Sir Richard Bingham, a colleague of Ralegh in the Smerwick executions, describing the subsequent fight at Ardnary in Connaught, says :—

"The number of their fighting men slain and drowned that day we estimated and numbered to be fourteen or fifteen hundred, besides boys, women, churls and children, which could not be so few, as so many more and upwards."

In stigmatising such acts, Mr. Froude refers to Sir Peter Carew "murdering women and children, and babies that had scarcely left the breast," and he adds :—

"The English nation was shuddering over the atrocities of the Duke of Alva. The children in the nurseries were being inflamed to patriotic rage and madness by tales of Spanish tyranny. Yet

Alva's

Alva's bloody sword never touched the young, the
defenceless, or those whose sex even dogs can
recognise and respect."*

XIV

Irish Council and Judges oppose Burghley's Policy

Burghley saw the evil consequences to England,
as well as to Ireland, of this anti-Irish policy.
But he stood almost alone.   At rare intervals and
in the earlier part of her reign Elizabeth supported
him.   Her officials in Ireland, however, obstructed
Burghley at every point.   In those days the Irish
judges were politicians as well as jurists.   In those
days the Irish Privy Council represented one
interest only.   The head of the judicial bench
spoke of the Prime Minister's suggestions of
pardons and remedial measures, as " agreeing to

* ' History of England,' vol. x. ch. 59, p. 251-2.

recompense

recompense felonious offences," and, instead, the
Lord Chancellor's policy was summed up in one
word, "hanging." Though there is something
more judicial in the halter than in the other
instrument of death, this representative of justice
in Ireland wrote a letter to Walsingham, in
which he expresses his opinion that it would " have
been better, if ten years past the Governor had
put on determination to subject the whole Irishry
to the sword." The members of the Irish Privy
Council were as much opposed to Burghley's views
as the judges, and so indeed were nearly all the
officials. From the permanent staff of Dublin
Castle, down to the newly appointed magistrates
in Kerry and Cork, there appeared to be a dogged
determination to act against the wishes of Burghley
and to rule Ireland by coercion alone. The com-
bination of the impolitic official element in Ireland
was too strong for the wise Lord Treasurer. Carefully selected Lord Deputies failed him. Secretaries that he sent to Dublin Castle armed with his
prudent counsel and their own good intentions,

gave

gave way to the dominating spirit of the Pale and
became coercionists.   He had no real Parliament,
no English press, no influential public opinion to
support him.   But though he could not carry his
policy, he lived long enough to see the Nemesis
that was coming.

XV

Ralegh's Agrarian Troubles

It is exactly three centuries since the sound
advice of one of England's best statesmen was swept
aside to make way for the selfish schemes of the
oligarchy of the Pale.   In vain he said do not
drive the Irish people from the soil; do not give
confiscated lands to individuals.   In his library at
Hatfield are recorded the first pages in that sad
complaint which has gone on from generation to
generation, now sinking and now rising, a chorus
of the oppressed and the oppressors.   Sir Walter
Ralegh was one of the first to feel the consequences

quences of his own injustice. The remnant of the
Irish peasants that escaped the sword had hardly
been forced to cross the Blackwater to the mountains and woods, leaving the fields of Desmond
to the new tenants from Devonshire, when the
grievances of the landlord reached the ear of Cecil.
The Lord Treasurer and the English Council had
received a significant report from the Commissioners for surveying the seigniories of the escheated
lands, dated from Youghal, October 1586. "At
Lismore and Youghal," they wrote, "we have
stayed these eight days in meeting and bounding
such lands as we hear Sir Walter Rawley is to
have, which hath been exceedingly difficult and
painful by reason that the lands having been
long waste, and generally overgrown with deep
grass, and in most places with heath, brambles,
and furze, whereby, and by the extremity of rain
and foul weather, we have been greatly hindered
in our proceeding; and, for that we find all
the gentlemen undertakers and their associates
that came hither to be again departed into England,
we

we surcease from further dealing therein until the spring."

The following year a rough survey was completed and Ralegh's courage and vigour enabled him to begin, in the words of his leases, "the repeopling of the Province of Munster." At first he murmured about the physical difficulties of reclearing the sort of secondary jungle that had sprung up on the removal of the old agricultural population. Any natives that came from the woods and mountains were unfriendly to the new settlers. Even when a sort of truce was proclaimed, and they were offered sustenance and wages instead of the rope, or the edge of the sword, Ralegh could not get them to assist in moving the timber his colonists cut down, or to do a stroke of useful work. This form of passive resistance embarrassed and annoyed the undertaker, who turned to the Government— what was called the Government—for a remedy. At first the Government tried to assist him. The refusal of workmen to do work was to be treated as a sort of treason. New schemes of coercion

were

were invented, but they did the settlers no good. Dublin Castle at length got tired of Ralegh's suggestions.

Ralegh then turned to England and complained of Dublin Castle. Whilst he could not get his own rents and profits, the trifling sum payable to the Crown was dragged from him by distress warrants, evictions and costly legal processes. His English are not protected by the Lord Deputy. The Lord Deputy encourages rebels to push out Englishmen from his castles and farms. The sheriff carries off five hundred milch kine from his people for an alleged debt of fifty marks which Ralegh believed he had paid, but which was not only enforced again but magnified into a debt of four hundred pounds. His poor Devon farmers are left without cattle in a strange country newly set down to build and plant. He and his colonists look around in vain for sympathy. The Irishry of the woods and bogs are no worse than the Dublin Castle agents. " The doting Deputy," he finally writes, " hath dispeopled me."

Ralegh's despairing cry might have been the echo

of

of the last words of the hunted Earl of Desmond, of whose penalties as well as of whose forfeitures, he seemed to be the political heir. Even at the other side of the Channel, the "Curse of Sherborne," as it was called, pursued him. When nothing of his vast Irish estates remained to him but the old Castle of Inchequin Ralegh, he writes to Cecil in 1603, of his other property :—

"My tenants refuse to pay my wife her rent. I hold divers leases uppon forfeture, in that mannor, of myne own tenants. Alas! all goes to ruin of that littell which remaynethe. My woods ar cutt down; my grounds wast; my stock—which made up my rent—sold. And except sume end be had, by your good favor to the Kinge, I perishe every waye.

"This I leve to your tyme and charetabell care, and rest your Lordship's miserabell poore frind, ever to be cummanded by yow,

"W. RALEGH.

"Of £3,000 a yeare ther remayns but £300; and uppon that £3,000 debt."

XVI

His Queenstown Estate

Burghley had seen that Ralegh's application for Irish lands was made in a spirit that boded ill for the future relations of the two kingdoms. Ralegh's letter to Sir Francis Walsingham of 1581, in which he asks for an estate, secretly denounces his general, the Earl of Ormond, for not being severe enough with the Irish. He begins by saying how he wished to occupy the Castle of Barry's Court and the adjoining island, "being a great strength and a safety for all passengers between Corke and Youghal," but the Earl of Ormond, "unwillinge any Inglishman should have anything, stayed the taking thereof." He then says: "I pray God her Majesty do not finde that she hathe spent a hundred thousand pounds more; she shall at last be driven by too dere experience to send an Inglishe President to follow

these

these malicious traytors with fier and sword." The English President he suggests in place of Ormond is his own kinsman, Sir Humphrey Gilbert. He then protests that his sole object is the love of the Queen and her service.

" I beseiche your Honor to take my bold writing in good part, protesting before Hyme that knoweth the thoughtes of all hartes that I writ nothing but moved thereto for the love I bere to her Highness and for the furtherance of her service."

A more substantial motive, however, appears in the closing sentences of the letter :—

"I beseich your Honor that I may by your means enjoy the keping of this Barre Court and the island; or that it will please your Honor to writ to my Lord Deputy that he will confirm it unto mee."

The Lord Deputy confirmed the grant, but Burghley advised the Queen not to sanction it.

This estate, which extended from Rostellan Castle to Fota, included one side of Cork harbour, and was coveted by Ralegh for many good reasons. He was a sailor as well as a colonist; and, if he

was

was fated to be the first colonial governor in America, and an administrator of an English colony in Munster, he was destined to be an admiral of the Royal Navy also. Hence his land hunger included not only a strong castle or two, but the idea of a residence near the sea, where he could have easy access to his ships, and where he could indulge his passion for mercantile speculation. Mr. Goldwin Smith, in his Oxford lectures, says : " The eagles took wing for the Spanish main ; the vultures descended upon Ireland." Ralegh seems to have united some of the characteristics of both.

XVII

His Blackwater Estate

Two years after he was deprived of Barre Court, and in little more than a year after his first expedition to America, he was a successful suitor to Queen Elizabeth for forty-two thousand acres in the province

province of Munster.   A marginal note in her own handwriting on the warrant attests the Queen's anxiety to hasten the completion of the grant. Amidst the foreign undertakers who were devouring the lands of the Earl of Desmond and the plunder of the Church, Ralegh evidently was the favourite, and was allowed to pick and choose.   He began at the "havan roiall" of Youghal, and at both sides of the river he took the best that could be found. Mr. Edwards says, "Ralegh's broad lands were thickly wooded;" and he surmises that this led him into a commercial speculation, which for many years gave him trouble, and involved him in eventual loss.

But there was something on this Blackwater property besides timber.   A man of Ralegh's literary and historic tastes cannot have been entirely insensible to traditions of intellectual culture, some of them then very recent.   From the upper windows of the house he occupied, close to the College of Earl Thomas, he could look across the river to his hills of Ardmore, which hid the *Cloig-theach*, one of the best preserved round towers

of

of Ireland. On this part of his property stood the Oratory of St. Declan, and the sculptured cathedral in which he might have seen the mysterious Ogham stones, that are perhaps the earliest efforts at writing in Western Europe. If any of the English undertakers noticed such antiquities, it should have been Ralegh, for the only Ogham stone found in England was discovered at Fardel in Devonshire, where his father was born. Molana Abbey, where Raymond le Gros is buried, was granted to Ralegh the year after the monastery was dissolved. In 1586 the Dominican Friary, that had been built in Youghal by Thomas Fitzmaurice Fitzgerald in 1268, was granted to Ralegh. During his mayoralty of Youghal in 1587 he ordered or allowed the destruction of this fine building, the massive piers and broken arches of which still remain. Ralegh's agents in the demolition, according to a book published in 1620, were unfortunate. " An Inglishman breaking down the monastrie of S. Dominiques in Youghull fell dead from the toppe of the Church, all his limmes being broken,

A.D.

A.D. 1587.   Also three soldiers which did cast
downe and burne the holye roode of that monastrie
died within one seanight after they had done it."*

The miraculous image of the Virgin, which made
this monastery famous throughout Europe, was
saved from Ralegh and his soldiers by the daughter
of one of the Geraldines whom he had pursued.
The silver case in which the beautiful ivory image
is preserved, bears this inscription :

"Orate pro anima Onoriæ filiæ Jacobi de
Geraldinus qæ. me fieri fecit.   Anno Dni. 1617."

From Ralegh's time to this there has been a
perpetual succession of Dominican custodians of
the ruined abbey and the sacred image, the Rev.
B. Russell of Cork being the present holder of
that office.

The Preceptory of the Knights Templars at
Rincrew and the confiscated lands of the order
were granted to Ralegh by letters-patent that are

---

* 'Theatre of Catholique and Protestant Religion,' p.
124, quoted by the Rev. S. Hayman.

still

still preserved in the Duke of Devonshire's archives
at Lismore.

XVIII

His Educational Policy

The reputation for learning, which made Lismore
known to European scholars before Oxford was
founded, may have induced Ralegh to select it as
a place for a school; but the school he˙endowed,
like others of later times, was a failure, because it
was avowedly established to destroy the faith of
the people.   Dr. Caulfield, in one of his valuable
contributions to Irish history,* quotes the original
grants of the Queen to Ralegh, including " the
patronage or gift of the wardenship of Our Lady's
College of Youghall."   Before Ralegh got it, the
Corporation of Youghal applied in vain for this
endowment, which the Queen at first decided

---

* Council Book of Youghal, xliv.

F   should

should be still employed "in the well bringing up of children in learning and the mayntance of others according to the foundation." But, beyond his selecting the warden's house for his own residence, no evidence can be found that Ralegh took any interest in saving or reviving the College. It had been a sort of Catholic University. Those who are interested in the history of Irish education can trace to this useful endowment of the Geraldines a little of the learning and classical taste that the Western Island assisted in diffusing in some parts of the Continent until the new school of Educationists arose in the reign of Elizabeth to reform and destroy.

It is easy to blame Ralegh for looking unmoved at the ruins of a Catholic University or sharing in its spoils. But, in this, he was controlled by the policy of Her Majesty's Government; a policy briefly summed up,—"we must put a stop to priestcraft and superstition in Ireland: we must take the responsibility of educating the Irish in our own way." In a few years he realised in his agrarian troubles

troubles some of the moral and social consequences of this imprudent policy.   For this he is more to be pitied than blamed : especially when we remember that what are called leading Catholic laymen have played a somewhat similar part as educationists in later times, and with a like result as regards their own comfort and the peace of their country.   He did not, however, trouble himself much with such questions.

XIX

The National Cause and the Land Question

The more one looks into the details of Ralegh's connection with Ireland, the more the accuracy of Mr. Lecky's statement is seen, that theological animosity did not then play the leading part in Irish history.   Ralegh's letters from Ireland also show the soundness of Mr. Lecky's judgment as to the slight importance attached at that time to nationalist views.   No doubt, eighty years later, the

policy

policy of Charles the First in Ireland, as Lord
Beaconsfield * has shown, by its recognition of an
independent Irish Parliament and a real Irish Executive, under the Crown, established for the moment,
what Thomas Davis would call a national conservative government.   But the elevating sentiment
of Nationality, the antidote, as Mr. Justin M'Carthy
observes,† to much that is unwholesome, vulgar,
and debasing, was overshadowed when Ralegh
was in Ireland.   The land question was the
dominating question of Ralegh's day.   It ruled him
from the moment he set foot in Ireland to the last
hour in which he was able to affect the fortunes or
misfortunes of the country.   Without mentioning
his name, Mr. Lecky indicates the real Ralegh
spirit when he speaks of the taste for adventure, the
dislike of routine, the extreme desire to find out
new and rapid paths to wealth, that characterised
the Elizabethan age—a desire showing itself in the

* Speech on the state of Ireland, Hansard's Debates,
February 16, 1844.
† 'Nineteenth Century,' March, 1880, p. 421.

form

form of discovery, of piracy, of a passion for Irish land. The Government policy was, as Mr. Lecky says, to root out the Irish from the soil, to confiscate the property of the septs, and plant the country with English tenants. He observes how Edmund Burke, in one of his letters to Sir Hercules Langrishe, gives the real clue to Irish history from the accession of Elizabeth, in asserting that the true genius and policy of the English Government was directed to the total extirpation of the interests of the natives in their own soil; that this was the original scheme, and that it was never deviated from for a single hour during the whole reign of Elizabeth. That Edmund Burke should have thus, in a passing remark, shown so exact an appreciation of the subject, Mr. Lecky attributes to his great intellect as well as to the fact that he studied Irish history with care. But the little boy that was reared at Castletown Roche, and Monanimy, on the banks of the Blackwater, where the estates of Ralegh came close to those of Spenser, and in the midst of a peasantry ever whispering of those days,

may

may possibly have picked up something in his uncle Nagle's house and in the school near Kilavullen more useful to him as a student of real history than what he afterwards found in the library of Trinity College.   Though in the days of Ralegh the land question thus dwarfed the religious and the purely national ones, it is impossible not to see that whatever influence the Catholic Church and the awakening national sentiment of Ireland could exercise, was a conservative influence in the truest sense of the word.   That influence was an influence on the side of order, of an ancient civilisation and of property, as opposed to the destructive policy of men like Ralegh—something that in course of time would enable a Sovereign who wields great moral power to use such words in writing to the Irish Bishops as "justam patriæ causam," and "publica populi Hiberni causa," whilst condemning un-hallowed societies, agrarian outrages, and the infamous practice of assassination.

XX

" *This Loste Land* "

If the literature of the Elizabethan age has been unrivalled, and the statesmanship of Burghley almost unrivalled, it must also be admitted that there never were so many Englishmen of commanding ability employed in the attempted subjugation of Ireland, as in the time of Ralegh. In the seven centuries of suffering, no Lord Lieutenants, Secretaries, Councillors, and Captains, can compare with such a group as Sussex, Sydney, Grey, Perrot, Mountjoy, Russell, Carew, Spenser and Ralegh. The commonplace mediocrities of later times have shared with those illustrious men good intentions to begin with, and despair to finish with. All alike have followed in the beaten track of the three steps, hope, coercion, failure. No Englishman in Ireland, in the long history of misrule, had greater self-reliance and

determination

determination than Ralegh. No one was more devoted to his Queen, or more sincerely resolved to make the Western Island a sort of flourishing outpost of Devon and Cornwall. With his master, Lord Grey, and his companion Spenser, he commences full of confidence. The confidence gives place to repressive measures, suited to the fashion of the age—women hanged, children put to the sword, Irish leaders poisoned by hired assassins. Lord Grey, after governing and struggling for years, writes to the Queen that he is ruined and the country is ruined, and he implores to be recalled. Ralegh sums it all up in three words, "this loste land!" A popular song of our own day describes in a single line current events as well as Spenser's 'State of Ireland,' and Ralegh's rule in Munster :

"The most distressful country that ever yet was seen!"

—distressful indeed, not alone because of seven hundred years of national pain, but because of the sad shipwreck of noble reputations, the judgments pronounced by each succeeding generation upon

upon the well-meaning British officials who earned the dislike of millions of poor people one day, and in the next the condemnation of their own historians and countrymen. What English historian now defends the Irish policy of Ralegh and Spenser? Who can turn without a pang from that page in the 'State of Ireland' in which the Lord Deputy's Secretary describes the thin faces of the Irish peasants, who were dying for want of food? Who does not feel a still sharper pang on reading how he welcomed the depopulation of the country as being the best for English rule? The shadow of Dublin Castle never fell upon a Secretary of gentler disposition, or finer genius. Centuries may pass before there can come another with such culture, and so refined a character, to behold, as Spenser did, the familiar scene of hunger-worn peasants, to take, as Spenser did, the responsibility of trying to rule a people he did not know.

XXI

Land Commission to fix Rents

The Irish land question undoubtedly puzzled Elizabeth's advisers. Projects without end were submitted to her. In the same volume of the State Papers for 1577, is a report from the Irish Chancellor to Walsingham referring to the "cruelty of the landlords," reducing the "tenants to be starved beggars," and a despatch from the Lord Deputy to the Queen, in Council, recommending "Commissioners to settle the rent, landlords shall take of their tenants,"* and also desiring "a Commission to compound for arrears." The undertakers constituted a sort of land corporation to substitute loyal tenants from England for what was left of the stubborn Irish. The land Commissioners fail, the arrears Commissioners fail, the

* State Papers—Ireland, vol. lvii. 5.

English

English tenants fail. Lord Burghley's two main ideas, that the lands should not be given to individuals, and that the remnant of the Irish should be encouraged to administer their own local affairs, were not tried; but the schemes of inferior men, sometimes of obscure and almost unknown persons, were welcomed by Elizabeth; reformation one day, extirpation the next. All experiments that had the character of national vivisection were encouraged, but all in vain.

XXII

Destruction of Irish Woods

In addition to the women and children, there were other helpless and innocent objects to be rooted out as enemies to Queen Elizabeth; and, as to these, no man cut down and destroyed more than Ralegh. In a letter addressed to Lord Burghley in the year 1588, Mr. George Longe urges

urges the Lord Treasurer to transfer to Ireland thirteen out of the fifteen glass manufactories then existing in England, for the reason that " the woods in England will be thereby preserved and the superfluous woods in Ireland wasted, than which in tyme of rebellion her Majestie hath no greater enemy there."*   Ralegh, actuated by a better motive, that of simply trying to make money, brought over bands of English woodcutters, and soon made short work of venerable groves of oak and yew trees, wherever the waterway of the Avondue and its tributaries could convey the lumber to his ships at Youghal. He obtained a monopoly for exporting pipe-staves to the Continent, and for some years the wines of France, Spain, and even Italy came to England in hogsheads of Irish wood.   Ralegh's letters and the Privy Council Records show that this destructive monopoly reacted upon him in reputation and in purse. It involved him in lawsuits, and in quarrels with

* Sir H. Ellis's ' Original Letters,' vol. iii. p. 159.

the

the Executive. But, like his political policy, it left its marks on the country. When Spenser first welcomed Ralegh to Kilcolman Castle, he says it was

"bordered with a wood
Of matchless hight, that seem'd the earth to disdaine,
In which all trees of honour stately stood."

In a few years not a tree was left, and the demesne that was described as "the woody Kilcoman" became a few naked fields surrounding the bare and burnt walls of the castle. And so throughout Cork, Kerry, Tipperary, and Waterford, Elizabeth's undertakers did their work. The cutting down of the Irish forests because they sheltered the Irishry is frequently mentioned in the State Papers of this period. What remained of the full-grown trees on Ralegh's former estates, were dealt with for a more legitimate purpose in the following reign. In a note in the Carew Papers by John Powey, ship carpenter, he gives the number of trees marked " along the river of Youghal " for the King's ships, in two months of 1611, as amounting to 7500 trees

trees to be felled. The ancient chroniclers who called Ireland *Fiodha Inis*, the island of the trees, did so not merely because it was well wooded by nature, but because the natives, at a time when little was known elsewhere of the advantages of tree-planting, fostered the art, and especially surrounded the numerous abbeys, the seats of religion and learning, with groves. Even Mr. Froude cannot read the testimony of one of Ralegh's comrades on this subject without drawing the contrast between the Irish "traitors" and the English undertakers. In Sir R. White's diary (1580) he says : "A fairer land the sun did never shine upon ; pity to see it lying waste in the hands of traitors ;" whereupon Mr. Froude observes : "Yet it was by those traitors that the woods, whose beauty they so admired, had been planted and fostered. Irish hands, unaided by English art or English wealth, had built Muckross and Innisfallen and Aghadoe."*

Whether or not Lord Burghley's correspondent

* 'History of England,' vol. xi. p. 225.

was

was right in saying that the Queen had no greater enemy than the Irish trees, their fate, at all events, showed the possibility of a physical destruction that time has been unable to repair. With the people the result has been different, though they were treated to a similar process by the same men.

XXIII

Burghley and Ralegh Anti-Papal

On one point only was Ralegh's policy in Ireland in entire accord with the views of the Prime Minister. No doubt when Burghley used the serious words Mr. Froude quotes, that the Irish had more cause to rebel against the tyranny of England than the Netherlanders against the tyranny of Spain, the Prime Minister had in his mind long years of severe repression, as well as the immediate proceedings of undertakers such as Ralegh. But whilst Burghley, like his brilliant successor

successor* of our day, could thus feel in a sort of
historical conscience a justification of Irish rebellion, he was, of all English premiers, with perhaps
one exception, the most determined enemy of
Vaticanism.   On the land question, the great
Cecil preferred a native proprietory to the system of
foreign undertakers and absentee landlords, which
he foresaw would involve chronic trouble to
England; but he was overruled.   He would have
yielded local self-government to the demands of
Hugh O'Neill, but his wise counsels were pushed
aside for those who boasted that they could establish
permanent order by never giving way to Irish
sentiment.   Nevertheless, he heartily supported
Ralegh and the Irish administration of that day in
priest-hunting.   When the undertakers cried out
that a hostile population was closing in upon them
and crimes of violence spreading, Burghley joined
with the others in saying, root out Popery.   When
Adam Loftus, the Protestant Archbishop, wrote to

* Mr. Disraeli : House of Commons, February 1844.

him

him that villages of English settlers in his diocese had been burned and the settlers murdered, and that his life was daily threatened by the recently formed secret associations of native assassins, the reply was, extirpate the old religion, and teach the Irish morality in your own way.

XXIV

The Last National Archbishop of Cashel

Ralegh was then in Ireland active in a career of cruelty. He had not then learnt the lesson he repeated in years to come, when writing those touching letters from the Tower, appealing to the mercy of James the First,—"Compassion hath ever bynn repayd with compassion, and cruelty with cruelty." When he so wrote he may perhaps have remembered his former letter to Robert Cecil, announcing the capture of Father John Mooney, "an Irishman and a notabell

G   stout

stout villayne," and the sort of "examination" he put him through: or he may, perhaps, have recollected with remorse the despatches from Dublin Castle about the Archbishop of Cashel, Dr. Hurley—how the Lords Justices wrote to Walsingham, "We have neither rack nor other engine of torture in Dublin Castle to terrify Dr. Hurley; the Tower of London would be a better place for his examination;" then in a few months, "We made commission to Mr. Secretary Fenton to put him to the torture, such as your Honour (Walsingham) advised us, which was to toast his feet against the fire with hot boots. We recommend he should now be executed by martial law, as the best lawyers doubt whether he can be found guilty of an offence against the law in Ireland:" * the native historians state that when one of the boots was taken off, the flesh came away, leaving the bones of the leg and foot bare.†

* State Papers—Ireland, vol. cviii. 8.
† Dr. Reneham's 'Lives of the Irish Archbishops,' vol. i. p. 254.

"As

"As he can hardly be convicted by a jurie," answers Walsingham, " hir majestie's pleasure is that you take a shorter way with him."* Finally comes the despatch from the Castle, reporting Dr. Hurley's execution without trial,—simply by order of Archbishop Loftus and Sir H. Wallop,— on the 17th of June, 1584.

Possibly Elizabeth agreed with Walsingham and Ralegh that all this "would teach a lesson," and that Dublin Castle would never be troubled again by a National Archbishop of Cashel. And yet when Ralegh was at Lismore with Sir George Carew, in September 1589, he might have heard it whispered how a man dressed like a poor peasant had passed on that way to Tipperary to kneel in the ruined chapel of Cormac, the successor of Archbishop Hurley, one of a long unbroken line, from that day to this, of Archbishops of Cashel.

* State Papers, vol. cxi. 12.

Ralegh opposes Mciler Magrath

The prelate referred to by Ralegh in his letter of May 1596 was not of this line. He was one of Elizabeth's creations, an Anti-Irish Irishman who reflected but little credit on the Queen or the Church of England. The State Papers contain ample evidence justifying Ralegh's account of him. Indeed, whatever fault may be found with Ralegh for his maltreatment of old educational endowments and his appropriation of Church lands, it must be admitted that his attempt to substitute Hugh Broughton for Archbishop Meiler Magrath in the see of Lismore, showed a sincere desire on Ralegh's part to promote the true interests of the newly created State Church, as opposed to the jobbery of ecclesiastics like Loftus and Magrath.

" The Archebishopp of Cashell," writes Ralegh, " is

" is a man whome I thinck my Lord Treasurer hathe little cause to favor... I doe fynde noe better meanes in releffe of my self, fartheraunce of relygon and comforte of all myne Inglyshe tenants and frendes, than in preferring some other of better sorte to the bishoppricke of Lesmore and Water-ferde wherof the Archbishop hathe but a commende, and hathe, besydes, twoe or three other bishoprickes." In place of Magrath, Ralegh suggests " Master Hugh Broughton, a man well knowen to all the lerned docters and scollers of Englande....a man able to do moche good and be a greate comforte to all our Inglishe nation thereaboughtes, and encrease of relygyon."

Ralegh's interest was powerful in England, but Magrath had secured the Irish Council. In the ninety-sixth volume of the State Papers for 1582, there are some characteristic memorials of the Archbishop : he suggests that, in certain cases, no judge, jury, or witness, should be allowed who had not taken the oath of supremacy. Soon after he goes further, and " wishes for authority to impose the

the oath of supremacy upon all manner of persons within the whole province of Cashel." He then prays for " the grant of the fee farm of the monastery of Tuam in Tipperary;" and about the same time he "desires the custodiam of all livings, except the bishopricks, in Ulster:" so that his ecclesiastical ambition stretched from one end of the island to the other. For half a century he held five bishopricks and many livings. But he had no flock. Sir Robert Cecil writes of him in 1600 as "a most turbulent spirit;" and in the following year he says, "Great scandal is bruited about the Archbishop of Cashel, that he doth very irreligiously suffer his church to lie like a hog-sty. Expostulate with him for the honor of Her Majesty and God's Church wherein he hath so supreme a calling."

In 1610 a Royal Warrant records the fact that "the Archbishop of Cashel is seldom resident upon his see, but absent in the north upon his own temporal lands." Before this however, the Archbishop had asked for protection to enable him to live

live in his diocese. So far from acknowledging him, the poor people had captured him and his three sons, maliciously broken the Great Seal from his letters-patent, and made him pay a heavy ransom for his liberation.

Between this prelate of the State Church and the disguised Archbishop who ministered to the people in woods and caves, there was certainly a contrast; but between Meiler Magrath and Ralegh's candidate for the see of Lismore there was almost as great a contrast. Hugh Broughton was an Englishman of high character, an eminent divine and one of the most famous scholars of the English Church. Elizabeth had him in her mind for the see of London. And yet, with all Ralegh's influence, he could not succeed in getting for Broughton one of the plundered sees out of the grasp of a man whose conduct so seriously compromised the English cause—such as it was.

XXVI

Ralegh's Testimony in the Lords in 1882

The House of Lords recently displayed unwonted interest at hearing the name of Sir Walter Ralegh repeatedly mentioned. It was in connection with his Irish estates. Under Elizabeth's grant he not only broke the ancient Celtic tenures throughout the domains of the Desmonds, but he usurped also the popular fisheries of the Blackwater. The rights of the attainted Earl, of his tenants and of the fishermen of Youghal, were all sold by Ralegh for a few hundred pounds to Mr. Richard Boyle, first Earl of Cork. This astute and successful planter escaped with his life from the clutches of Lord Strafford to found, on the estates of Ralegh, more than one great house. His memory as a resident despot is to this day not cherished by the people, whilst, strange to say, his chief descendants

are

are popular absentees.   On the death of the fourth
Earl of Cork in 1753, the Lismore and Youghal
estates went to Lady Charlotte Boyle, the wife of
the fourth Duke of Devonshire.   After long litiga-
tion, the House of Lords finally decided in the last
session that Sir Walter Ralegh's grant conveyed to
the present Duke of Devonshire an absolute right
of salmon fishing in the tidal waters of the Youghal
river to the exclusion of the natural rights of the
public.   No one can blame the Duke for termi-
nating by law a long dispute.   The decision was
based on the sweeping terms of the Queen's grant
to Ralegh, as interpreted by English law.   In that
point of view it is sound and indisputable.   But
according to the customs that prevailed before the
estates of the Geraldines came to Ralegh, it is
alleged that there were popular privileges of fishing which the Desmonds, at the very height of
their princely power, could not have taken from the
people.   From time to time, the inherent right of
gathering food from the tidal waters was exercised
by the common fishermen, though often disputed
by

by the landlord.   At length, three hundred years after it was signed, the deed of Elizabeth was brought back again from Lismore to London, and the shade of Ralegh came as it were to the Bar of the House of Lords in 1882, to testify against the claims of the Irishry.   But whatever may be the historic interest of the decision, those who live on the banks of the Blackwater know that the just and kindly Cavendishes will not use the now established rights of Ralegh to the injury of the poor.

XXVII

Ralegh and Cromwell

Mr. Froude has reminded us more than once of what Sir Walter Ralegh's first master, Lord Grey, said, that the only way to deal with Ireland was by "a Mahometan conquest."   In the 'Nineteenth Century' for September 1880, Mr. Froude again refers to Lord Grey's suggestion as "a cruel but in the

the long run merciful one," if Ireland is to be kept
in subjection. Indeed, the historian has never
disguised his bias in favour of a system of unrelenting severity and a bold attempt at extermina-
tion. Had Cromwell lived, he has often told us,
the experiment would have been worked out. But
he has hardly done justice to the great Protector
or to the difficulties in his way. Long before his
death Cromwell had realised the impossibility of
exterminating a nation. He had tried it, but
failed. Nor has our unrivalled historian done justice to his own favourite theme, for he overlooked
the fact that his experiment had been previously
tried, and, as far as it was possible, thoroughly tried.
It was tried under circumstances the most favourable for its success, and such as never can occur
again. It was tried by a man of genius, daring
and no scruples—by a man who did not stand
alone, but, with his resolute companions was
backed up by whatever force England could afford.
It was tried at a time more likely to insure success
than in the days of Cromwell—at a time when

novel

novel improvements had been effected in the art of
war and new weapons had been brought into use,
but improvements and weapons employed, as
Ralegh himself tells us, for some years by one side
only. The man who, with these advantages, was
able to try the experiment was not open to the
imputation that Mr. Froude lays against the
Geraldines and the still later Boyles and Cavendishes, that with their Irish estates they acquired
some Irish feeling, and did not look at Ireland
from a purely English point of view only. Mr.
Edward Edwards says (vol. i. p. 320) :—

" With the interests of Ireland, indeed, Ralegh
gave himself no trouble. He looked at Irish affairs
just as his fellow-soldiers and fellow-councillors
looked at them, with preoccupations exclusively
English. In Ireland he was an English soldier,
and an English planter, and he was nothing more.
. . . His face was set as flint against peddling
interferences and temporary expedients in dealing
with great evils. To cut the tap root rather than
to spend precious time in pruning the branches was

his

his maxim. And it may well be that occasionally he pressed it unduly."

Here was a man to Mr. Froude's heart. He not only wielded the sword himself, but, having gained the ear of his Queen by the thoroughness of his Irish policy, he never wavered in advising her to maintain undeviating severity, and the despotic ruler acted upon that advice. The wise Lord Treasurer had to submit in silence, and see the Mahometan system tried by this bold and vigorous captain and his martial-law companions—not tried by fits and starts, or for a few years only, but tried as persistently as they could do it and over a long period. The reign of Queen Elizabeth was not a short one. From the time when the Lord Deputy Sussex arranged with her for the assassination of John O'Neill down to her last interview with Ralegh was a period of forty years. During that time the only servants she rewarded for work in Ireland were the Mahometan-conquest ones. It was not victories she rewarded so much as severity and the effort to exterminate. Sussex with his hired

hired assassins and poisoners, was a failure, but still he was rewarded. Ormond was recalled by her from Ireland, and the second Essex ruined, partly because Ralegh whispered that they mingled some thought of Irish interests in the English work she had given to them. Mr. Froude's suggestion in favour of the policy of Cromwell would hardly be approved by the shade of Elizabeth's great Minister, if in the tomb he could hear it ; nor would it be approved by the Minister of a truer woman and a better Queen, who, writing from Hughenden Manor in October 1870, said : " Ireland should be governed according to the policy of Charles the First, and not of Oliver Cromwell."*

* Mr. Disraeli's Preface to his collected works, 1870.

XXVIII

Ralegh and Ormond

Mr. Froude quotes Ormond's indignant letter to Burghley :

" My Lord, the clause in the Queen's letter seems most strange to me. I will never use treachery to any, for it will both touch her Highness's honour too much and mine own credit ; and whosoever gave the Queen advice thus to write to me is fitter to execute such base service than I am. Saving my duty to her Majesty, I would I were to have revenge by my sword of any man that thus persuaded the Queen to write to me."

Ralegh was then at Court. His letters written from Cork in 1580 and 1581, secretly denouncing his general for not using the fire and sword enough, had gained him the Queen's regard before the romantic incidents of the velvet cloak and the lines
written

written with the diamond ring upon the window
occurred—or were invented. Ormond, it might
be thought, was as unrelenting and thorough as
Mr. Froude could wish, but he was not prepared
to go quite as far as the Gilberts and Carews, to
get the Irish to come in from the woods and mountains of Duhallow under pledges of protection for
their lives, and then, seizing them unprepared, to
hang them up, as Ralegh did, from the North Gate
bridge to the Red Abbey of Cork. Mr. Froude's
comment upon Ormond's letter of 1583 points,
in a few words, the contrast between him and
the English captains to whose charge Ireland
was for so many years entrusted by Elizabeth :
" To Ormond the Irish were human beings with
human rights. To the English they were vermin
to be cleared off the earth by any means that
offered."*

Amongst the draft charges to be laid against the
Earl of Ormond, was one to the effect that two

* Froude's ' History of England,' vol. xi. p. 258.

assassins

assassins, hired by the Lord Lieutenant to murder
Fitzgerald, the seneschal of Imokilly, were stopped
and exposed by Ormond. That traitors should be
prosecuted by the hired dagger was not agreeable
to Ormond; and his private conversations denouncing the practice were reported to the Privy
Council by Ralegh. The following is the passage
in the Carew Papers, volume 607, page 71, from the
articles against Ormond:

" Where two choice persons were entertained for
the killing of the traitor Seneschal, and had undertaken the same, the matter not being revealed to
any by the persons that entertained them, saving
only to the Earl of Ormond, these executioners
were no sooner arrived at the camp but they were
apprehended by the Seneschal, and charged with
the practice, and for the same executed, to the
great grief of the persons that entertained them.

"Let Captain Bartley and Captain Rawley be
examined of words privately uttered by the Lord
General (Ormond) touching the prosecution of
traitors. Persons to prove those articles: Sir

H   George

George Bowcer, Sir William Morgan, Captain
Bartley, and Captain Rawley."

XXIX

Irish Self-government

Sir John Perrott also experienced the adverse
influence of Ralegh. He complains bitterly of
Ralegh's opposition to him. As one of the leading
gentlemen of the Pale, Ralegh supported his
repressive measures, but opposed him in other
things. The idea of giving real freedom to an
Irish Parliament was not consistent with Ralegh's
Irish policy. Few historians have noticed the
fact that, at one moment in Elizabeth's reign, this
all-important step was nearly taken.

Here again the oligarchy of the Pale defeated a
wise project, and the Lord Deputy found the
permanent staff of the Castle intriguing against the
idea of an independent legislature for Ireland. A
Bill

Bill for the repeal of Poyning's Act was duly certified by the Speaker of the Irish House of Commons
in April 1585. On the 30th of May, Sir John
Perrot writes to Walsingham : "There is no good
meaning in the people of the Pale and borderers
towards the composition intended, or anything else
that is good. They have overthrown the repeal
of Poyning's Act."* The historian Cox also attributes the defeat on the third reading of the Bill
for repealing Poyning's Act, to the "jealousy of
some gentlemen of the Pale."† Indeed any plan
that an enlightened English statesman might have
had for giving to the Irish the responsibility of
administering the affairs of their own country, was
not likely to meet with much favour from the
gentlemen of the Pale, and especially from that
inner circle of the Pale composed of the judges and
officials, with whom at that time Ralegh was
cordially working.

* State Papers, Ireland, vol. cxvi. 69.
† Cox's 'Reign of Elizabeth,' p. 384.

H 2 XXX

XXX

Florence McCarthy

Ralegh's letter to Cecil of the 4th of March, 1593, throws some light on a disputed point in Irish history,—the true character of Florence McCarthy. Ralegh knew him well. He met him as a boy in 1580. They corresponded on Irish affairs; and when Elizabeth welcomed McCarthy to London he and Ralegh were frequent companions at Court. The Celtic chief was being played off against the Norman Geraldines, until his romantic wedding offended the Queen. Elizabeth was planning an alliance between one of her officials in Munster and an Irish heiress, the Earl of Clancar's daughter, when Florence suddenly left London for his native county and married the lady in spite of the Lord President's guards. For this the young bridegroom got his first experience

of

of a State prison, in which he was, at different times, to spend over forty years. Long after his ill-starred marriage, for Cecil employed the wife as a spy upon the husband, Ralegh thus writes of him :—

"Florence MacCarty is a man reconciled to the Pope, dangerous to the present State, beloved of such as seek the ruine of the Realme." He adds,—" He is not worthie to be relieved by her Majesties goodness. He may for a time dissemble, by occasion of his imprisonment in the Tower ; but he is not to be trusted."

From his own point of view, Ralegh was doubtless right in his estimate of McCarthy, who, in spite of his early training at Court, was a patriot at heart,—"a man infinitely adored in Munster," as one of the Queen's officers, in denouncing him, records.

The reference to Florence, in Ralegh's letter of October 1601, also shows a true appreciation of McCarthy's influence. Relying on their old friendship and the literary tastes they had in common,

common, Florence, over and over again, writes to
Cecil to refer his case to Ralegh's judgment. He
was in fact appealing to that judgment at the very
moment that Sir Walter was privately objecting to
the contemplated pardon.

On the unwise but constantly recurring theory
that peace and prosperity were alone to be secured
by keeping Ireland down and governing her by
Englishmen, Ralegh was justified in recommending
Cecil not to let Florence McCarthy out of the
Tower. Had Perrot's idea of a local Parliament
with real powers been carried out, Florence
McCarthy would have been a leader in the Irish
House of Commons, the true friend of both
kingdoms. He was a scholar, a man of enlightened views, and of a winning disposition. Like
his old friend and political foe, he was a historian.
Ralegh, who was one of the main agents in his
imprisonment, became again his intimate companion
in after-years. When he himself passed through
the Traitors' Gate he found McCarthy in a cell,
surrounded with books and manuscripts, writing

his

his 'Treatise on the Antiquity and History of the
Early Ages of Ireland.' McCarthy's History was
preserved in his clear and minute handwriting for
two centuries and a half, till it was edited and
published by the late Dr. O'Donovan.

XXXI

His Last Advice to the Queen

Another of that Celtic clan felt the weight of
his influence. Having referred to the consistency
with which Ralegh counselled the Queen to maintain an unrelenting demeanour towards the Irish,
from the first word she heard him utter in 1582 to
the last time she saw him in 1602, Mr. Edwards
goes on to say how he did this alike in open
conference with the Queen and in his private
advice to her Ministers. He refers to his last
recorded interview with Elizabeth about three
months before her fatal illness. The question was,
what

what should be done with respect to Cormac Mac-Dermod McCarthy, Lord of Muskerry. Cecil in his letter to Sir George Carew of November 4, 1602, mentions how he reported to her Highness that the President of Munster had already spoiled the country and taken the castles of Cormac. In his previous despatch from Cork, dated October 25, 1602, Carew reported how the towns had been burnt, and there were " killed and hanged divers poor men, women, and children appertaining to Cormocke." The fire and sword had swept from Carrigrohan to Inchigeelagh. The Queen heard again the words which for over forty years had been so often repeated at her Council table : " The rebels' country is utterly spoiled." Cecil thought some mercy might be shown to the hunted chief whose people were slain and whose castles were ruined, but he tells how the Queen turned to Sir Walter Ralegh. "Whereupon Sir Walter very earnestly moved her Highness to reject Cormac MacCarthy." He gave the old and sufficient reason, " because his country was worth her keeping."

keeping." The Queen, he adds, was "so wrought upon by Ralegh's advice as to give special charge about the next despatches to Munster : no pardon should be given to Cormac MacCarthy."

Such was Ralegh's last advice to Elizabeth. In a few months another sovereign was on the throne, and before long the friends of Ormond and of Essex were reminding the new King that the gallant Captain of the Guard had little scruples about the shedding of blood.

XXXII

The Emigration and Re-peopling Plans

In the lease made by Sir Walter Ralegh in 1588, and now to be seen in his house at Youghal,* he describes himself as "one of the principal under-takers with Her Majesty for the repeopling of the

---

* Appendix.

land

land in the counties of Cork and Waterford."
One of the main conditions on which he and the
other undertakers got the confiscated estates, was
that this repeopling should be by persons of English
birth only, and that no Irish should be allowed to
remain on the lands. It was not for any want of
zeal or energy that Ralegh failed in this cardinal
point of the undertaking. He had for eight years
co-operated with Mackworth, Zouch, and Carew,
in removing the Irish peasants from their own
soil. Though the sword and the halter were freely
used, the other two weapons for clearing the
country, famine and emigration, were not neglected. The emigration which was promoted by
Dublin Castle and its agents in the Tudor period
was not across the Atlantic. The noble colonies,
whose birth will ever be associated with the genius
of Ralegh, had not become the new home of a
formidable section of the Celtic race. The gallant
captains who got the lands did their best to clear
off the people, one of Ralegh's friends recording
how they starved to death 30,000 in six months in
the

the province of Munster by destroying the crops.*
But the State Papers of that day contain suggestions
from more benevolent-minded persons in England,
who thought emigration was the true remedy, but
emigration across the Blackwater, and to the woods
and mountains of Kerry. In any shape or form,
however, the Irish race do not like emigration.
Those who benevolently promoted the transfer of
the people from the once fertile ploughlands of
the Geraldines and the MacCarthys to the back-
woods beyond the Pale, were as little loved by the
poor emigrants as the Captains who pursued them
in a rougher style. In their new homes among the
mountains they remembered the fields where they
had been born. By a sort of instinct which the
foreign rulers were quite unable to comprehend,
these dispossessed farmers looked upon the few
well-intentioned and benevolent emigrationists much
in the same light as they looked upon their enemies
who wielded other weapons. Hence the emigration

* Sir Warham Sentleger to the Queen, from Cork, 1582,
vol. xci. 41.

did

did not work well, and Ralegh soon found a
double difficulty in his repeopling scheme.

In spite of the desolation described by Edmund
Spenser, some Irish had survived in the vast
districts where none but English were to live in
future. This tempted the undertakers to break their
engagements with the Government, as they thought
the remnant of the hunted people might be utilised
in again tilling the ground. The Lord Deputy
could not understand this. Commissions were
issued to inquire if any of the Irishry had been
allowed to remain. The undertakers who con-
nived at the breach of engagement were worried
by the Castle.

On the other hand, from the rugged colonies of
the emigrant race, there came messages and agents
of disaffection. The Curfew Act failed to check the
growth of midnight outrages. The lessons of
assassination that Sussex, Carew, and Ralegh had
taught the people began to be practised by both
sides. From the distant mountain that Edmund
Spenser has immortalised—

" . . . that

> "... that mountain gray,
> That walls the north side of Armulla dale"

—there dropped down, one by one, active fomentors of trouble, until at length the gentle poet, but perhaps too severe soldier, fled broken-hearted from Kilcolman, whose roof (which had often sheltered Ralegh) he beheld for the last time in flames. "My undertakers," writes the Queen to the Lord President of Munster, "either for lack of comfort from you or out of mere cowardice, fled away from the rebels upon the first alarm." Elizabeth's emigration scheme and Ralegh's re-peopling scheme failed, having done more harm than good, as sometimes happens with well-meaning plans framed by one people for the management of another people.

XXXIII

Dedication of the Irish Wars

And here the question may perhaps be asked, how comes it that Mr. Froude tells us nothing of Ralegh's doings in Ireland and of his Irish policy? The one vague reference to him as having accompanied Lord Grey to the west of Ireland in 1580, is all he tells us about Ralegh. Mr. Froude says not a word about his being for twenty years the favourite adviser of the Queen on Irish affairs; not a word about the special training she desired, under her royal warrant of February 1582, that he should continue to receive in Irish affairs; not a word about his successful intrigue against Ormond, and barely a word about the reward he got of forty-two thousand acres in Munster. Of his doings as Deputy President of Munster, as Governor of Cork, as Mayor of Youghal, as the daring leader of the English

English soldiers in many a raid from the mouth of the Blackwater to the sources of the Lee, Mr. Froude is also silent. But on the last and not least important point—the result of the policy so recommended and enforced—Mr. Froude speaks out. " The entire province of Munster," he says, " was utterly depopulated. Hecatombs of helpless creatures, the aged, and the sick, and the blind, the young mother and the babe at her breast, had fallen under the English sword; and though the authentic details of the struggle have been forgotten, the memory of a vague horror remains imprinted in the national traditions."

The contemporary chronicle, Hooker's Supplement to Holinshed, which is so often quoted by Mr. Froude, describes all this and gloats over it as a notable and rare example of a people being justly rooted out, as the true and rational settlement of the Irish difficulty. Hooker appropriately dedicates his record of those Irish wars to Sir Walter Ralegh, on the ground that the " right worthie and honorable gentleman and knight" was " a partie and a

dooer

dooer, a painful and a faithful servitor" in those trans-
actions, the effect of which he thus sums up in the
same 'Epistle Dedicatorie :'—"The common people
such as escaped the sword all for the most part are
perished with famine or fled the countrie. The
land itself, from beinge verie fertile, is waxed barren,
yeelding nor corne nor fruits—the pastures without
cattell : nothing there to be seene but miserie and
desolation."

XXXIV

The National Traditions

Here then was Mr. Froude's system tried. All succeeding efforts in that direction were less thorough.
The " curse of Cromwell," the broken treaty of 1691,
the way an insurrection was produced and punished
in 1798, the means employed to repress local self-
government in 1800, the coercive legislation that
followed,—these were of the same character, no
doubt, but less thorough. They have, however,
served

served to stereotype that vague horror which Mr. Froude tells us remains in the traditions of the people of Ireland.

Are those terrible traditions all that remain of Ralegh's days in Ireland? How long are they to remain? What has been their effect in a country where the two main elements of social order—the religion of the people and the national sentiment —have not been allowed to play their legitimate part in the Government? Are those traditions growing, as political agents, less powerful with the increasing strength of popular spirit in Europe? How far does a frank admission of their vitality and their force enable us to look into the future?

Spenser and Ralegh

Some of these are questions for practical politicians to consider who either hold the helm or aspire to do so. A mere student of history must be content to answer the first question only and to turn to the more pleasing reminiscences of Ralegh—to think of him wandering with Lord Grey's Secretary beneath "the green alders by the Mulla's shore" or sitting in the deep embrasured window of the Warden's house reading the manuscript of his brother poet and then " æmuling " the pipe of Spenser, who tells us

> "His song was all a lamentable lay
> Of great unkindnesse, and of usage hard:"

the unkindness of the Queen who in some jealous fit had exiled him to his Irish estates—to the country which

which he had contributed to render not "a common wealth but common woe." The advice he gave to Spenser in the old house in Youghal and in the spoiled and desolate fields of Desmond was an event in English literature.

> "When thus our pipes we both had wearied well
>   (Quoth he), and each an end of singing made,
> He gan to cast great lyking to my lore,
>   And great dislyking to my lucklesse lot,
> That banisht had my selfe, like wight forlore,
>   Into that waste, where I was quite forgot.
> The which to leave, thenceforthe he counseld mee."

The noble sonnet that Ralegh then wrote, in which he says—

> "All suddenly I saw the Fairy Queen,
> At whose approach the soul of Petrarch wept"—

and the sound advice he gave Spenser, well earned for him the immortal distinction of the dedication written in Kilcoman Castle,—

> "To thee, that art the summer's nightingale,
>   Thy Sovereign Goddess's most dear delight,
> Why do I send this rustic madrigal,
>   That may thy tuneful ear unseason quite?

I 2   Thou,

Thou, only, fit this argument to write,
In whose high thoughts Pleasure hath built
   her bower,
And dainty Love learnt sweetly to indite."

Indeed that dedication was due to him, to his literary genius, to his critical taste, to his encouragement of the exiled poet, as much as the dedication by Hooker of the Chronicles of Ireland had been won by his sword and halter.

It is evident from Spenser's testimony that a good deal of Ralegh's poetry was written in Ireland. In some of his pathetic verses there are traces of his Irish exile. He was, however, so pre-eminent as a man of action, that he is underrated, or almost forgotten, as a poet. Spenser indeed was justified in writing at Kilcolman in 1591,—

"Full sweetly tempered is that Muse of his."

XXXVI

Introduces Tobacco and the Potato

The richly-perfumed yellow wallflowers that he brought to Ireland from the Azores, and the Affane cherry, are still found where he first planted them by the Blackwater. Some cedars he brought to Cork are to this day growing, according to the local historian, Mr. John George MacCarthy, at a place called Tivoli. The four venerable yew-trees, whose branches have grown and intermingled into a sort of summer-house thatch, are pointed out as having sheltered Ralegh when he first smoked tobacco in his Youghal garden. In that garden he also planted tobacco. The climate of the south of Ireland favoured its cultivation. Many years after his time the name of Ralegh was favourably mentioned in College Green, when the Irish House of Commons contemplated encouraging tobacco plantations

plantations in Ireland. The supposed necessity, however, of protecting tobacco planters in the colonies and supporting the customs revenue of England compelled the Lord Lieutenant to veto any revival of Ralegh's scheme.

A few steps further on, where the town wall of the thirteenth century bounds the garden of the Warden's house, is the famous spot where the first Irish potato was planted by him. In that garden he gave the tubers to the ancestor of the present Lord Southwell, by whom they were spread throughout the province of Munster. In an old book of travels in the northern countries, quoted in the 'Gentleman's Magazine' eighty years ago, it is said, "Potatoes were first planted here (in Lancashire), having been brought from Ireland to England by the immortal Ralegh." Writing from Cork in August 1602, Carew says to Sir Robert Cecil, "I sent unto Sir W. R. many sorts of ore. I would be glad to know how they prove, and that speedily." Before this, Ralegh had brought some Cornish miners to Ireland, and had spent a considerable sum in

trying

trying to develope the mineral resources of the country. How different would the popular traditions respecting Ralegh in Ireland be, if his taste in such things and his literary genius had been associated with a wiser and more truly English policy than that of repression !

XXXVII

The Old Countess of Desmond

He himself recalled Irish memories sometimes unaccountably. In his great folio he illustrates the long lives of the patriarchs by his own knowledge of a lady who lived about five miles from Youghal. "I myself," he says, "knew the old Countess of Desmond of Inchiquin in Munster, who lived in the year 1589 and many years since, who was married in Edward the Fourth's time, and held her jointure from all Earls of Desmond since then ; and that this is true all the noblemen and gentlemen of Munster

Munster can witness."   This lady, the Countess Catherine of Desmond, was born in 1464, the year in which the eighth Earl built Sir Walter Ralegh's house.   In a letter written after he had sold his Irish estates to Mr. Boyle, he says : " There remains unto me but an old castle and demesne which are yet in the occupation of the old Countess of Desmond for her jointure."   From this it would appear that she was then one hundred and thirty-eight years of age.

In his Youghal house can now be seen two original documents that throw some light on the controversy as to this lady's age.   One is Sir Walter's lease sealed by him on the 21st of July, 1588, of a small neighbouring property, in which he refers to " the Ladie Cattllyn old Countess Dowager of Desmond;" the other the original warrant of Queen Elizabeth dated 2nd October, 1588, with the Royal autograph and signet granting a pension to Eleanor, widow of the 16th Earl of Desmond.*   Sir

* See Appendix.

George

George Lewis and others thought that the passage in Ralegh's 'History of the World' must have been hastily written, and that the old Countess could not have been alive in 1589. Sir Walter's deed, however, shows that she was undoubtedly living, five miles from his Youghal house, in 1588. In that deed he calls her the "old Countess." It was known that a Countess of Desmond had walked in 1587 from Bristol to London to petition the Queen for a pension, and it was said she could not have been so very old if she were capable of such exertion. Sir George Lewis thought this conclusive against the alleged great age of the Countess. But, as the Queen's original warrant now seems to establish, it was not the Countess Catherine, but the Countess Eleanor who walked from Bristol to London in 1587.

XXXVIII

The Two Widows

In one of Ralegh's letters to the Lord Deputy, he accuses Ormond of parleying with the Countess of Desmond, allowing her to leave Cork with many followers, and "at her going away none of her trayne either searched or lokt over." This was the Countess Eleanor, who, a few years before, was the wife of Elizabeth's wealthiest subject, a correspondent of the Queen, a lady of "princely castles and fair gardens," and whose "gown of cloth of gold" is referred to in one of the letters to Burghley in January 1579. Ormond no doubt remembered her former state, and what was due to her sex and rank, when he allowed her to pass without being searched, especially when her husband, his bitter foe and political rival, though not yet killed, was hopelessly ruined. In a short time the widow had

had a graver complaint to make against Ralegh than want of gallantry. He had got a share of the Desmond estates, and the jointure lands of the Countess Eleanor were taken. When Ralegh was full of hope with his repeopling schemes, with the fame and fortune he was to win in his Irish colony, the evicted Countess thus writes to Burghley :—

"I am enforced through extreme poverty to make my moan unto your Honor. At this present my misery is such that my five children and myself liveth in all want of meat, drink and clothes, having no house nor dwelling wherein I with them may rest."*

Whilst Ralegh was holding his mayoralty in the house at Youghal, one of the last of the Desmond buildings that sheltered the widow before the undertakers drove her out, she sent a memorial to the Queen saying,—

"Until Sir John Perrott came, I remained in most extreme want and misery : myself and my

* State Papers—Ireland, vol. cxxii. 68.

poor

poor children were almost famished, whereupon the
Lord Deputy sent us a dish of meat from his own
table." After that, she adds, " My Lord Ormond
paid for my diets." The head of the rival family !
Again she petitions the sovereign that of her late
husband's vast estates and her own jointure lands,
not a blade of grass is left to her.

One of Burghley's last acts was to advise the
Queen to give a pension of £200 a year to the
Countess. The Royal Warrant to that effect, with
the bold autograph of Elizabeth upon it, is, with
some other original papers, in the old house at
Youghal. But there is no evidence either in
Ireland, or in the State Paper Office, that Ralegh
had assisted the widow whose estate he held. It
is only fair, however, to remember that the Queen
gave her this pension when Ralegh's court influence was at its height, and that he was constantly
consulted on Irish affairs.

It was the fate of another widow to cry out as
poor Lady Desmond did. In her petition to
King James the First, Lady Ralegh said :—

" I

"I beseich your majestie, in the mercies of
Jesus Christ, to signifie your gracious pleasure
concerning myselfe, and my poore children: That
whereas your majesty hath disposed of all my
husband's estates, so that there remayneth nothing to give me and my children bred."

The widow and her son, Carew Ralegh, attempted in vain to oust Sir Richard Boyle from
the old Desmond estates. At one moment
Carew Ralegh's prayer seemed likely to succeed.
Lord Cork was charged by Wentworth with
having possessed himself of the estates by chicane.
But the Lord Chief Justice, in denouncing Lord
Cork for "depopulating" the College of Youghal,
spoke in the same letter of the lands and endowments "torn from the Church by the poure of Sir
Walter Ralegh."

Neither of the widows could regain an acre of
the lands their husbands had held. But after
much petitioning each secured a pension. In the
Patent Rolls of the 7th of James the First is recorded a grant of "£400 per annum, in trust to

Sir

Sir Francis Darcy and Sir Nicholas Throgmorton, during the life of Elizabeth Lady Ralegh." Her pension was larger than Lady Desmond's. But the English widow was granted another special favour she valued very highly. She was allowed to embalm Sir Walter's head, and she carried it about with her wherever she travelled. At her death it was left to Carew Ralegh, in whose coffin it was ultimately buried. The Irish widow, if she had had a similar sad devotion, would have had to take up her lodgings in one of the old houses on London Bridge.

XXXIX

Ralegh opposes Essex's Irish Policy

One part of Ralegh's Irish policy which affected his own fate and contributed to the apparently never-ending troubles of the two kingdoms, was his successful opposition to the conciliatory schemes of the second Essex. It was rumoured that

that the Queen had offered Ralegh the post of
Deputy before Essex was sent to Dublin. However that may be, Ralegh was her most intimate
adviser on Irish affairs during the Lord Lieutenancy
of Essex.

The new Lord Lieutenant and Ralegh had
been bosom friends, had quarrelled and had made
it up again. From the day when Essex had
cast his plumed hat into the sea to greet Ralegh
before Cadiz, there had arisen many causes of
jealousy. But the alternate smiles and frowns
of the Queen were as nothing compared to their
divergent views on Ireland.

The Irish manuscripts known as the Annals of
the Four Masters, speak of Essex as having displayed "the most splendid regal state ever
exhibited by the Saxons in Ireland." As to his
Irish policy they say, "When the Earl of Essex
arrived, the first thing proclaimed was that every
one of the Irish who was sorry for having gone in
opposition to the Queen should receive forgiveness,
that any of the men of Ireland whose estates had
been

been taken by the Saxons through oppression, violence or illegality, would have a restitution of the same." No wonder the undertakers should determine to trip up a Lord Lieutenant whose views were so interpreted by the natives.

The first journal of Essex's proceedings that reached the Queen described his march through the counties where Ralegh's estates lay. The latter read with surprise how "the Lord Lieutenant summoned the castle of Darrilayrie. The rebels surrendered and were pardoned." "Rebels pardoned!" That was not the way Ralegh dealt with traitors in those districts eighteen years ago. Then in a despatch from Essex dated July 1599 came a few words that Elizabeth and her advisers started at. "This poor country of Ireland!" But more serious than words of commiseration were the instructions from the Governor in Dublin Castle to those generally severe and intriguing politicians, the Irish judges, to "treat the Irish people with caution and tenderness. To refrain from laying any heavy burthen upon them, or taking any severe course

course against them. To avoid making them desperate."* Then followed stories that Essex was countenancing Popery;—all culminating in his interview and treaty with Tyrone, in which complete toleration to the Catholic religion, and, what would have been in effect, Irish self-government under the crown of the Queen, appear to have been agreed upon.

The trenchant style of Ralegh can be detected in the Queen's answers, censuring and destroying the plans of Essex. "Your pen," she writes to him, "flatters you with phrases, that you are disgraced from hence, that 'poor Ireland' suffers in you. We will not tolerate this." And in a more official despatch to the Lord Lieutenant in Council, she tells him : "Your opinions deserve reproof rather than answer. . . . You have been the cause of corruption in religion by favouring Popery." As to Essex's agreement with the gallant Hugh O'Neill, Elizabeth writes : "To trust this

* Essex's instructions to Judge Saxey. 'Carew MSS.,' vol. 607, p. 143.

K   raitor

traitor upon oath is to trust a devil upon his religion."

Essex, who had been for so many years the companion and correspondent of Ralegh, recognised the hand that guided the Royal pen. Replying from Ireland, he said, " Is it not known that from England I receive nothing but discomfort and soul's wounds? Is it not lamented of your Majesty's faithfullest subjects, both here and there, that a Cobham and a Ralegh should have such credit and favour with your Majesty ? "

Mr. Edwards, who is not free from what Lord Macaulay calls the disease of biographers, supports the Irish policy of Ralegh as against that of Essex. "Ralegh," he says, "was repeatedly consulted about Irish affairs both by the Queen and by her Ministers. His advice was uniformly in favour of measures vigorous and decided. In his view, the submission of rebels was the essential condition precedent of their reconciliation. That view Ralegh had always taken. It was the Earl of Essex's misfortune that he did not take it too."

When

When Essex imprudently returned to the Court to defend his Irish policy in person, he found Ralegh at the Queen's ear. For a moment Essex seemed to win Elizabeth. Ralph Adderley writing to Walter Bagot on the 9th of June, 1600, says, " Ralegh is gone into the country, bag and baggage, wife and children. Her Majesty called him worse than cat and dog." Then came bad news from Ireland, and Ralegh was welcomed again at Court. At the trial he was a witness against Essex, when the latter exclaimed, "What bootheth it to swear this fox ? "

It seems to have escaped the attention of Ralegh's biographers that though the subtle Lord High Treasurer, as Naughton calls Burghley, was no longer living in 1599, he had recorded, in 1595, a paper concerning the Earl of Tyrone in which is to be found more of the conciliatory views of Essex than the so-called vigorous views of Ralegh.* Had Burghley a Lord Lieutenant like Essex, or had

---

* ' Carew Papers,' vol. 614, p. 237.

Essex

Essex the support of a Prime Minister like Burghley, the relations of the two kingdoms would have been different. Ralegh's fate might have been different also, for in his temporary triumph over Essex it is possible to trace some of the steps that brought him to a similar end. Standing by the block in 1618 Ralegh's final words were :—

"It is said I was a persecutor of my Lord of Essex : that I puffed out tobacco in disdain when he was on the scaffold. But I take God to witness I shed tears for him when he died. I confess I was of a contrary faction. But I knew he was a noble gentleman. Those that set me up against him, did afterwards set themselves against me."

XL

" Destiney stronger than Councell "

As the popular traditions of Munster may furnish some notes for an unwritten chapter of Ralegh's and Spenser's Irish life, a fact which Professor Hales, the latest biographer of Spenser, has recognised, so, in the State Paper Office in London there may also be found an unprinted history that throws some light on this "contrary faction" to which Ralegh belonged. It was the anti-Irish faction in the Court and Councils of Elizabeth. The biographers of Essex still keep speculating on the mystery surrounding his fall, instead of turning to the mass of Irish correspondence now available to writers and students. For the months of remorse, the worry and sleepless nights that preceded the death of Elizabeth, ample material can also be found in that unpublished history

history. One day the Queen adopts Ralegh's advice; the next day he is in disgrace. Then in a sort of despair she calls him back again, to read another batch of Irish despatches. Many years had passed since Ralegh told her how Ireland could be held, by vigorous measures, without any cost to her exchequer. He had gone on repeating that the true policy was to uphold the " Inglishe inhabitants in Ireland which are yet stronge enough to master the Irishe without any charge to the Queen." She acted on his advice ; and now, after forty years of repression, she finds Ireland more Irish than ever, more costly to her treasury, and kept down by the largest army of occupation that any English sovereign had sent across the seas. Though Ralegh had foreseen something of this,— though in 1593 he had written—

" That accursed kingdome hath always bynn but as a trafique for which Her Majestye hath paid both fraight and costome, and others received the merchandize ; and other than such shall it never be."

though

though in the same letter he had said,—

" A million hath bynn spent by Her Majestye in Irland. A better kingdome might have bynn purchased att a less price."

and though he had added,—

" Destiney is stronger than councell "—

yet he continued to advise the sending of more soldiers and the wasting of more money. Up to the hour of the Queen's death he continued to pit his counsel against the destiny that destroyed Elizabeth's Irish policy and was to overwhelm himself.

Though the unpublished documents in the Rolls Office relating to Ireland tend to compromise the reputation of Elizabeth's statesmen, they contain during a subsequent period of eighty or ninety years some records of a very different character. The Irish policy of the Stuart kings was halting and defective. But it was perfection itself compared to what had preceded it and what followed it. The early years in that glimmering of justice and common-sense brought some hope to Ireland and corresponding disaster to Ralegh.

The

The curious mixture in misfortune of Ralegh and his Geraldine victims can hardly have escaped his own notice in the Tower. He knew that the son of the sixteenth Earl, whose lands he held, was kept in the Tower till his health broke down, when the Queen gave him rank as seventeenth Earl for about a year before his premature death. This young lord's legitimate successor, and cousin, James, the eighteenth Earl of Desmond, was Ralegh's fellow-prisoner for some years.* Political prisoners in those times were not strictly confined to separate cells except at night. When Ralegh, in 1604, wrote to the Secretary of State, Lord Cranborne, from the Tower, "remember my miserabell estate,—dayly in danger of death by the palsey, nightly of suffocation by wasted lungs, And now the plaug cum here.. .. my poore child having lien next to a woman with a plaug sore, whose child this Thursday is dead of the plaug,"— he saw that he shared all this suffering and danger

* Appendix.

in

in common with the head of the Munster Geraldines.
Perhaps it was the daily presence of the wasting
Earl, for in 1608 he was buried in that historic
dust that Lord Macaulay has described, that
induced Ralegh in another letter from the Tower
to say :—

" Wee shalbe judged as wee judge—and bee
dealt withál, as wee deal with others in this life—
if wee beleve God Hyme sealf."

XLI

On the Scaffold

No one in Ireland seems to have deplored the
unjust execution of Ralegh.   The mass of the
Irishry remembered, what it has been the fate of so
many British officials to leave in the memory of the
people, repressive measures only.   But even in
what was then simply a garrison of the Pale, the
City of Cork, with its close corporation at that time

of

of English undertakers and their descendants, he
had no sympathisers.   The Meads and Coppingers,
who had formerly applauded his severe rule, now
found fault with him because the coercion they
had cried out for had reacted injuriously upon
themselves.   A premature rumour of Ralegh's
death reached Cork in 1603.   John Walley writes
from Shandon to Sir George Carew :—

"The Mayor and Recorder of Cork say his
lordship and Sir Walter Ralegh were both killed,
and were they living they should never command
there again as of old."

They were not very grateful for the way he had
risked his life in defending the city, and disposing
of their Irish enemies, a few years before.

The night before the scaffold something made
him think of Ireland.   In a paper endorsed by Sir
Thomas Wilson, the keeper of the Tower, "A copy
of the note written by Sir Walter Ralegh, in his
owne hand, which he gave me in discharge of his
conscience," is the following :—

"There is a lease in controversy betweene the Lord
Boyle

Boyle and one Henry Pine of the castle and lands of Mogile in the country of Corck in Ireland ; and although I did write something at my going from Ireland towards Guiana to the prejudice of Pine's lease, yet since that time better bethinking myself, I desire that the opinion which I gave of Pine's lesse may be no evidence in law against Pine, but that it may be left to other proofs on both sides."

This simple reference, at such a moment, to his long-lost Irish estates is pathetic, and, though on a trivial matter, it is something to record that his last thought of Ireland was one of reparation for an accidental injustice.

XLII

His Irish Residences

Of Ralegh's Irish residences, the old castle in Cork is gone, and on the spot where he wrote despatches to Walsingham and Cecil there now stand the prosaic warerooms of one of the members

for

for the city ; the Barre Court of his day is gone
and the island he held for a short time is
now Queenstown ; the Lismore Castle where the
popular Duke of Devonshire and Lord Hartington
occasionally visit and administer the estate in a
very different spirit from Ralegh's, is not, except in
its foundation stones, the castle of the fifteenth
century. Kilcolman Castle is a roofless, ivy-clad
ruin on the well-managed property of a descendant
of the Barrys with whom Ralegh fought ; but no
alders can now be seen on the banks of the Mulla.
The only house in which he lived that has survived the burnings, reprisals, and destructive raids
that swept away so many buildings in Ireland, is
the Warden's house of the College of Youghal, to
which he took a fancy because of its resemblance
to the old manorhouse at East Budleigh, where he
was born. When Mr. Crofton Croker sixty years
ago visited Youghal, he thus described it :—

" The house of the ill-fated Sir Walter Ralegh,
who was mayor of the town in 1588, is still to be
seen nearly in the same state as when inhabited by
him

him; and many objects are pointed out to which the charm of traditional anecdote is attached. It is long and low, the exterior plain and heavy, resembling the common English manorhouse of his time. In the interior those rooms which we saw were completely lined with small oaken panels, and had large wooden chimney pieces, embellished with very beautiful carved work."

Thomas Dyneley, in Charles the Second's reign, notices " the well wrought ancient chimney pieces " and the " extrem pleasant garden." But the most accurate description of Ralegh's house is that published in 1852 by the Rev. Samuel Hayman, the historiographer of Youghal. He speaks of the solid mementos of the fifteenth century, the walls five feet thick, the deep projecting bay window and porch, the orieled closet, the high-pointed gables and gablets, and the great towering chimneys.

"A large dining-room" (he says) "is on the ground floor, from which is a subterranean passage connecting the house with the old tower of St. Mary's Church

Church. In one of the kitchens the ancient wide arched fireplace remains. The walls are in great part wainscoted with Irish oak. The drawing-room —Sir Walter's study—retains most of its ancient beauty in the preservation of its fine dark wainscot, deep projecting windows, and richly carved oak mantelpiece rising in the full pride of Elizabethan style to the height of the ceiling. The cornice rests upon three figures, representing Faith, Hope, and Charity, between which are enriched circular-headed panels, and a variety of emblematical devices fill up the rest of the structure. In the adjoining bedroom is another mantelpiece of oak, barbarously painted over. The Dutch tiles of the fireplace are about four inches square, with various devices inscribed in a circular border. Behind the wainscoting of this room, a recess was a few years ago revealed in which a part of the old monkish library, hidden at the period of the Reformation, was discovered."

Some of the books Mr. Hayman describes may have been gifts to the Warden from James, the ninth Earl, and Maurice, the tenth Earl of Desmond, both

both of whom supported and enriched the educational foundation of their great ancestor, the good Earl Thomas. But one of the fifteenth-century volumes, Peter Comestor's 'Historia Scolastica,' is quoted by Sir Walter Ralegh in the second book of the first part of his 'History of the World.' In the same recess was also found a black-letter volume, printed at Mantua in 1479, of scriptural events in the history of the world from the Creation to the days of the Apostles. The elder Disraeli has argued that Ralegh could not have written the whole of his erudite folio himself, because he had not the books of reference in the Tower of London. But the discovery of one of the first editions of Comestor, and the black-letter epitome of early historical events, in the little recess in his Youghal bedroom, may indicate the possibility that Ralegh had been taking notes from the remnant of the Desmond library for the *opus magnum* during his frequent Irish exiles.

XLIII

Irish Portraits of Ralegh

In appearance, what manner of man was Ralegh when in Ireland? There was much change, of course, from the dashing captain of eight-and-twenty, when he was putting the unarmed men to the sword and hanging the women in Dingle Bay, to the admiral of sixty-five, who, between the Tower and the scaffold, visited his old haunts in the county of Cork for the last time in the three summer months of 1617. But all accounts agree in giving him a commanding presence, a handsome and well-compacted figure, a forehead rather too high ; the lower part of his face, though partly hidden by the moustache and peaked beard, showing rare resolution. His portrait, a life-sized head, painted when he was Mayor of Youghal, was recently presented to the owner of his house, where it had

been

been years ago, by the senior member for the
county of Waterford; and another original picture
of him when in Ireland is in the possession of
the Rev. Pierce W. Drew of Youghal.   Both these
Irish pictures show the same lofty brow and firm lips.
At Ballynatray is a full-length painting of Ralegh by
Zucchero.   In a corner of his Youghal house is an
engraving by Vander Werff of Amsterdam that seems
to combine all his characteristic features—the ex-
traordinarily high forehead, the intelligent eyes,
the same large but well-shaped nose, the moustache
and peaked beard, ill concealing a too determined
mouth.   The likeness is most striking.   But there
are accessories in this old engraving that seem
to indentify it, even more than the mere resemblance of the features, with Ralegh's career in
Ireland.   The knightly personage in armour is
shrouded in the skin of a wolf; the wolf's head
shows its sharp fangs at the top of the picture;
two human skulls are beneath, the eyeless sockets
of one being directed upwards to the portrait, with
an expression, as far as a poor skull can have

L   expression,

expression, of reproach and woe. Both skulls rest on the torch and sword, the dagger of the assassin and the halter. Surely that must be Ralegh? Examining it closer, however, it is found to be but the picture of one of his contemporaries and rivals in glory, Ferdinand of Toledo, the foreign coercionist of the Netherlands.

XLIV

Retrospect of Ralegh's Irish Policy

Looking back upon Ralegh's connection with Ireland, it is impossible to forget that he and Sir George Carew taught, by their example, the odious crime of assassination; but, with this exception, there is much that may be forgiven, partly because the " cruelty that is repayd with cruelty " was the general fashion of the day, partly because of the earnest efforts he made to develope the industrial resources of the country, and no doubt also because of the sympathy evoked by the literary and romantic

romantic side of his character, as well as the natural indignation one feels at his unjust end.

But his successful opposition to Perrot and Essex, on two main points, condemns him as the deliberate enemy of Ireland, and the unconscious enemy of England. Had he not assisted the oligarchy in stopping the repeal of Poyning's Act, had he not counselled the rejection of the Tyrone and Essex treaty, how different might have been the relations of the two kingdoms! Perhaps if he had supported Perrot and Essex on those two points, no possessor of his Irish estates, from the days of the ever-worried and anxious Richard Boyle to later times, would have had to declare that the Irish problem was the most important and the most difficult for English statesmen to deal with. In truth, it would seem as if the poor Irish-speaking peasants of Munster have not greater reason to complain of Ralegh, than the millions of perplexed Englishmen who love fair play and peace.

LETTERS OF SIR WALTER RALEGH FROM IRELAND, OR RELATING TO IRISH AFFAIRS.

To the right honorable and my very good Lord, the Lord
BURGHLEY, *Lord Highe Thresourer of England.*

MAYE IT PLEASE YOUR HONOR,

To UNDERSTAND that uppon the receaving
of my footeband of one hondrethe men, when I
departed from London towards this land, there
was then delivered into my hands (besides one
hundreth powndes in imprest which is defalked
uppon my enterteynment heere,) so muche mony
as amownted to six dayes wages for my self, my
levetennent, officers, and soldiers, at accustomed
rates, viz. iiij⁵ *per diem* for my self, ij⁵ *per diem* for
my levetennente, xiiijᵈ a peece for iiij officers,
and viijᵈ a peece for every soldier; after th' expira-
cion of which six dayes (by order from Your
Honor and the rest of my lords of Her Maiesties
Pryvy Counsell,) wee entered into the Isle of
Wighte where wee contynued xv dayes, and ther
beinge imbarked in Her Maiesties shippes, there

was

was xvii dayes more before wee arryved heere,
duringe all which tyme of xxxij dayes, in the whole,
wee receaved only vittells after the rate of vi^d
sterlinge *per diem* for eache one, so that duringe those
xxxij dayes there growethe due to every of my
company ij^d sterlinge *per diem* as a remaynder of
theire wages at viij^d sterling *per diem;* and also
to my selfe, my levetennente and officers, our
whole enterteynment for the lyke tyme at the
rates abovesaid.   So yt is, my goode and honorable Lorde, that at the importunate suyte and ex-
clamacion of my company I have bin enforced to
paye and satisfye every of them of that remaynder,
and seekinge to have the same to be allowed mee
agayne heere, I am therfore referred to Your
Honor's order and the residue of my Lords of Her
Maiesties Pryvy Councell in England ; being ann-
swered by Her Highnes' offycers heere that wee
are neyther to be entered into paye, nor no other
manner of waye to be allowed heere, but from the
daye of our arryvall in this land.   In consideration
whereof I am a moste humble sutor to Your Honor
and

and the residue of my said Lords for allowance of that mony, as hathe bin heretofore, by Your Lordship's good meanes, in the like case allowed to Sir WILLIAM MORGAN, and that the same may be payd to the gentleman which shall deliver this letter to Your Honor, whom I have desired to attend your Lordship for that purpose, and who shall present unto You as well a perfect accompte thereof, as also a suffycient certifycate or testemony of the tyme of our contynuaunce in the Wighte, and of the daye of our arryvall heere. I moste humblie desire Your honor to farther this my request as spedely as you conveniently maye, because I have appointed the mony to be imployed in England abowte the providinge of sutche wants as bothe my selfe and company doe greatly stand in neede of. Thus I comyt Your Lordship to God; my poore selfe remayninge alwayes at Your Honor's service and comaundment. Corke, this 22 of February, 1580.

Your Lordship's most humble to comaunde,

W. RAULEY.

II

To the honorable Sir FRANCIS WALSINGHAM, *Knighte, Principal Secretory to Her Highnes, geve thes.*

I RECEVED of late a letter from Your Honor wherein I finde Your Honor's disposicion and oppinion more favorable then I can anyway deserve. Notwithstandinge I hope Your Honor shall finde that my forwardnes to advance her Maiesties service shall not be less accordinge to my smale strenght. Whereas of late a cumpany of yonge cumpanions linket together in rebellion who because they can no longer covertly assiste the proclaymed traytors do at length manifeste their good mindes to Her Hightnes and the Inglyshe nacion,—as DAVY BARREY, sonn and heir of Lorde BARREY, now in the castle of Develin ; MORRICE ROCHE, eldest sonn to the Lorde ROCHE ; FINNIN MACARTEY, PATRICK CONNDON, and divers others,—my Lorde Generall

is

is now cum hither who, wee hope, ether by force
or pollecy will sufficiently hampre them that are
farr of greater strenght than the Earle of DESMOND
and JOHNE. In my returne from Develin I made
a hard escape from the Seneshall in BARRE's
countre (wher he is allways fostered) with xiiij
horsmen and threescore footmen.

I was three horsmen, and soun set on horsbake
to Irishe footmen. I coveted to recover a litle
old castle, and in that resun I left three men and
three horses. The manner of myne own behavior
I leve to the report of others, but the escape was
strange to all men. The castle was a longe mile
of, from the place wher he first sett on us. Ther
is great need of a supply in Munstre, for the bandes
ar all miche decayed. The bands of TANNER and
BARNISHE were so ordered in the cashiringe that
no man was the better. For the officers had the
furniture and the soldiers ran away. Beside, the
men ar suche poore and misserable cretures as ther
captaynes dare not lead them to serve. If Your
Honors beheld them when they arive here, You
would

would think them far unfitt to fight for Her Maiesties crown; and like Your Honor ther is no fit
place to lande them that ther captaynes may receve
them furnished but Corke, from whence they may
most conveniently be delivered over. Thus, besechinge You to continew Youre favorable oppinion
of mee, I humblie take my leve, restinge allways
most redy to do you all honor and service. From
Corke, xxiij of February, 1581.

Your honor's most humble to cummande,

W. RAULEY.

Endorsed :
"23 *February*, 1580. *From Mr. Walter Rawley.*"

III

THE day after the writinge of my letter to your Honor by Levetenant BIGGES, news came that DAVY BARREY had broken and burnt all his castles and entred publikly into the action of rebellion. It plesed my Lorde Deputy, att my beinge at Develin (forseinge wherunto this Trator was bent) to bestow on mee the kepinge of on of his castles called Barre Court and the Iland adjoyninge therunto; which hows he gave mee in charge to keap to her Majesties use, being a great strenght to the countre and a safty for all passingers betwen Corke and Youghall. Notwithstandinge, becaus my Lord Generall was presently to cum up and BARREY ready to go out (having before undreground broken the foundacions of the rest of his castles)

I

I made stay to take this Barrey Court, as well for
that my Lord Generall should not alledge that I
crost hyme in any service or did anythinge with in
his goverment without his privitey, as also because
it should not be sayd that the takinge therof was
the hasteninge of BARRE's rebellion. But when
my Lord came and BARREY had burnt all the rest,
the Lord Generall, ether meninge to kepe it for
hyme selfe—as I think all is to litle for hyme—or
els unwillinge any Inglishman should have any
thing, stayd the taking therof so longe, mening to
put a gard of his own in it, as it is, withe the rest,
defaced and spoled. I pray God Her Majesty do
not finde, that—what with the defence of his own
countre assalted on all sides, what with the beringe
and forberinge of his kindred, as all thes traytors
of this new rebellion ar his own cussen-germayns,
what by reason of the incomperable hatred betwen
hyme and the GARAUTINES who will rather dy a
thowsand deathes, entre into a million of mischeifes
and seek soccor of all nacions, rather than they will
ever be subdued by a BUTLER—that aftre Her
Majesty

Majesty hathe spent a hundred thowsand pound more she shall at last be driven by to dere experience to send an Inglishe Presedent to follow thes mallicious traytors with fier and sword, nether respectinge the aliance nor the nacion. Would God your Honor and her Majesty, as well as my poore selfe, undrestoode how pitifully the service here goethe forward! Considering that this man, havinge now byn Lord Generall of Munstre now about too yeares, theire ar at this instant a thowsand traytors more then ther were the first day. Would God the service of Sir HUMFRY GILBERT might be rightly lokt into ; who, with the third part of the garreson now in Ireland, ended a rebellion not miche inferior to this, in to monethes! Or would God his own behavior were suche in peace as it did not make his good service forgotten and hold hyme from the preferment he is worthy of! I take God to wittenes I speake it not for affection but to discharge my duty to Her Majesty; for I never hard nor rede of any man more fered then he is amonge the Irishe nacion. And I do
assuredly

assuredly know that the best about the Earle of
DESMOND, ye ! and all the unbridled traytors of thes
partes, would cum in hyre, and yeld them selves to the
Queen's mercy, were it but known that he were cum
amonge them. The end shall prove this to be trew.

And for myne own part God is my judge it
grevethe mee to receve her Majesty's pay (although
God knowes it be but a poore entreteynment) to see
her so miche abused ; and I will rather begg then
live here to indure it. I would most willingly geve
over my charge, and did offre it to the Lord Generall,
God is my judge, if I could, and serve her Majesty
privatly with a dussen or ten horse duringe the
wares. I beseiche your Honor to take my bold
writing in good part, protesting befor Hyme that
knowethe the thoughtes of all hartes, that I writ
nothing but moved therunto for the love I bere to
her Highnes and for the furtherance of her service.
And further I humblie crave at your Honor's handes
that you will reserve my letters to yourselfe, and if
your Honor will promise mee so miche and give
mee leve, I will from tyme to tyme advertise your
Honor

Honor trewly of this estat. Myself being on that your Honor shall allways finde most ready to ventur my life to do yow all honor and service during my life. I beseich your Honor that I may by your means injoy the keping of this Barrey Court and the Iland; or that it will please your Honor but to writ to my Lorde Deputy that he will confirm it unto mee, whom I find most willing to do mee any good, being my honerable, good Lorde. This humblie I take my leve, reposing myselfe and my estat uppon your Honors favor.

From Corke, the 25th of February.

Your Honor's most humble ever to command,

W. RAULEY.

Endorsed : " 1 May, 1581. *Copie of a letter to the Lord Deputy, from Corke.*

FERING that it shoulde seme strainge unto your Lordshipe the litle service don in thes partes, I presume to wryte unto your honor in myne owne excuse, lest your Lordshipe should growe in ill opinion of us that ar and have byne in the presenc of the General to be directed. The bandes of Sir GEORG BOWSER, EDWARD BARKLEY, Captayne DOWDALL, and of my self, have bine ever since the seconde weeke of Lent remayning in Corke ; and both the great wood of Conoloathe, Harlo, Clenlis, and all the countye of Lymbricke, and the counties betwene the Dingle and Kilkeny, left without any companies either to defend itself or anoy the enemy. Since which tyme wee have made to jurneys : the one towards Kilkeny to give convoye

to

to my Lorde and attend his returne, and the other into Conolothe, by which jurnes (the one being in horible wether, and the other utterly botles, being don without draught or espiall, and beside inforst to walke such unreasonable marches as, wher wee dispatched a churell of the traytors, wee lamed, lost, or left behynde unserviceable, a soldier or two of our owne) the poore bands have curste the change they made in levyng to follow your Honor, as they have tould the Lorde Generall many tymes. And this fyrst of May wee ar going another posting convoy towards Kilkeny. But to culler the matter, wee shall march some two dayes out of our way to seeke wee know not whome. The store of Corke, except it be a smale quantitie of wheat and butter, is all spent within the walles, and now it wilbe aleged that wee cannot serve for want of vittles, or else because the bandes ar not supplied ; allthough wee were nevere less than fore hundred stronge, and yet both of Sir GEORGE BOWCER's and Captain BARKLE's left at Kilmalloch and Asketon. Wee have spent thes two monethes of the spring in

M 2 parles

parles with BARREY ROWE, the Countes of
DESMOND, and FINNIN MACARTEY; and wee think
it willbe two moneth more er he be resolved
whether thes oughtt to be followed or no, and yet
theris no day passeth without some trayterous
villanies by the BARRES committed. The Countes
of DESMONDE is retourned, and brought so many
followers with her hither to carrye provision with
her as the Earle, for his parte, shall be the better able
to keepe the feild all this sommer; and at her going
away none of her trayne ether sercht or lokt over.
BARREY ROWE is protected. The Lady BARREY having gathered her goodes into Corke; and fering that
by the atteyndure of her husband those wilbe found
for the Queene, her yonge sonne—viz. BARRIE
ROE, that five dayes before fell on the garrisons of
Youghal—is brought in to serve that turne to carye
the goodes into O SYLLEVANSES countrey, or elswher, for the more saftie; and besides this man shall
keep some store of cattell and such impotent people
as cannot follow DAVEY BARREY in the feild with
many other profits ether for the Queen or for the
knaves.

knaves. I thinke your Honor hard of the losse of the warde of Asketon.* O KENIS and his sonn wer both slayne by JHON of DESMOND,—gentelmen of MAC DONOTH's countrey and very good subiects. Barre's Cowrte and the Iland—which your Honor willed me to keepe—the on hath sinc bin many tymes defaced, and the other spoylde and pred. From this iland the traytors can never wante nether wine nor salte, or iron, or any other necessary provision, or if neede bee advertisement from Spayne or elswher; being common for any man to lande on. Notwithstanding, it is left naked and the castle broken that stood in the entranc therof for defenc. I have, by great perswacion of the Commissioners, gott leve to edifie the same, and leve a ward therin; and if it shall please your Honor to thinke mee woorthie the keeping and custodie therof I will at myne owne coast buyld it up agayne and defend it for her Maiestie. I would the rather bee an humble and ernest suter to your

---

* " xi of them were distressed that fondly aventured owte to far for sum cowes."—*Marginal note by the Lord Deputy.*

Honor

Honor for it in that I heire the Lord Generall purposeth, when I have taken the toyle in making it defencible and bin at the charg, to turne me over for my charges to the Queene and dispose of the iland to some other. I hope your Honor will stand my good lord therin. If it please your Honor to give commission ther may bee an other hundreth soldier layd uppon the cuntre heire aboute.* I hope it willbe a most honorable matter for your Lordshipe, most acceptable to her Maiestie, and profitable for the cuntre ; and the ryght meane to banish all idle and frutles galliglas and kerne, the ministers of all miseryes. Thus, most humblie beseeching your Honor not to condemne any of us that are willing to deserve your Lordshipps good favor, I humblie take my leve. From Corke, the fyrst of May.

Copie of . . . . [Captain Rauley's]

letter (*the name being in cypher*).

* "This is the beeginnyng of that platt which, by Mr. Fent, I have advertizement of, for the fynding of a certayne garrison gratis to Her Majestie."—*Marginal note by the Lord Deputy.*

V

To the right honorable and my very good Lorde the Erle of LEYCESTER, *of her Majesties most honorable Pryvey Counsell.*

I MAY not forgett continually to put your Honor in mind of my affection unto your Lordshipe, havinge to the worlde bothe professed and protested the same. Your Honor, havinge no use of such poore followers, hathe utterly forgotten mee. Notwith-standinge, if your Lordshipe shall please to thinke mee your's, as I am, I wilbe found as redy, and dare do as miche in your service, as any man you may cummande ; and do, nether, so miche dispaire of my self but that I may be somway able to performe as miche.

I have spent some time here under the Deputy, in suche poore place and charge, as, were it not for that I knew him to be on of yours, I would disdayn

it

it as miche as to keap sheepe. I will not troble your Honor with the bussiness of this loste lande; for that Sir WARRAM SENTLEGER can best of any man deliver unto your Lordshipe the good, the badd, the mischeifs, the meanes to amend, and all in all of this common welthe, or rather common woo. He hopethe to finde your Honor his assured good Lorde, and your Honor may most assuredly cummande him. He is lovingly inclyned toward your Honor. And your Lordshipe shall win by your favor towards hyme a wise, faythfull, and valient gentleman, whos worde and deede your Honor shall ever find to be on.

Thus, having no other matter, but only to desire the continuance of your Honor's favor, I humblie take my leve. From the Camp of Leismore, in Irland, August 25 1581.

Your Honor's faithful and obedient,

W. RAULEY.

I am bold, being bound by very conscience, to cummend unto your Honor's consideration the pitiful

pitiful estate of JOHN FITTS-EDMONDS, of Cloyne, a gentleman, and the only man untucht and proved tru to the Queen, bothe in this and the last Rebellion. Sir Warram can declare his service, what he is, and what he deservethe.

VI

To my lovinge Cussen, Sir GEORGE CAREW, *Master of the Ordinance in Irland.*

CUSSEN GEORGE,

FOR my retrait from the Court it was uppon good cause to take order for my prize. If in Irlande they thincke that I am not worth the respectinge they shall mich deceave them sealvs. I am in place to be beleved nor inferrior to any man, to plesure or displesure the greatest; and my oppinion is so received and beleved as I can anger the best of them. And, therfore, if the Deputy be not as reddy to steed mee as I have bynn to defend hyme,—be it att is may.

When Sir WILLIAM FITZWILLIAMS shalbe in Ingland, I take mysealfe farr his better by the honorable offices I hold, as also by that nireness to her Majestye which still I injoy, and never more.

I

I am willinge to continew towards hyme all frindly offices, and I doubt not of the like frome hyme, as well towards mee as my frinds. This mich I desire he should understand; and, for my part, ther shalbe nothinge wantinge that becummeth a frinde; nether can I but hold myself most kindly dealt withall heretherto, of which I desire the continuance. I have deserved all his curteses in the hiest degree.

For the sute of Lesmore, I will shortly send over order from the Queen for a dismis of their cavelacions; and so, I pray, deale as the matter may be respeted for a tyme; aad cummend mee to Mr. Sollicitor with many thancks for his frindly deling therin; and I assure yow, on myne honor, I have deservde it att his hands in place wher it may most steed hyme.

For HARDINGE, I will send unto yow mony by exchange with all possible spead, as well to pay hyme (if he suffer the recoverye) as all others; and till then, I pray, if my builders want, supply them.

I look for yow here this springe, and, if possible

I

I may, I will returne with yow. The Queen thincks that GEORGE CAREW longes to see her; and therfore see her. Farewell, noble GEORGE, my chosen frind and kinsman, from whom nor tyme, nor fortune, nor adversity, shall ever sever mee.

The 27 of December [1589].

W. RALEGH.

VII

*To my honorable frinde, Sir R. CICILL, Knt., of Her
Majesty's most honorable Privy Councell.*

SIR,

I WRAT unto your father how I am dealt
withall by the Deputye, to whom my disgraces
have bynn highly cummended. Hee supposed a
debt of four hundred pounds to the Queen, for
rent, and sent order to the Shiriff to take away all
the cattell my tenants had, and sell them the next
day, unless the money weare payd the same day.
All Munster hath scarce so mich mony in it; and
the debt was indeed but fifty marks, which was
payde, and it was the first and only rent that hath
yet bynn payd by any undertaker. But the
Shirife did as he was cummanded, and tooke away
five hundred milch kine from the poor people;
sume had but two, and sume three, to releve their

poore

poore wives and children, and in a strang country
newly sett downe to builde and plant. Hee hath
forcible thrust mee out of possession of a Castell,
because it is in law between mee and his cousin
WINCKFELD, and will not here my atornes speake.
Hee hath admitted a ward, and geven it his man,
of a Castell which is the Queen's, and hath bynn
by mee new built and planted with Inglishe, this
five years; and to profitt his man with a ward-
shipp, looseth her Majesties inheritance, and would
plant the cussen of a rebell in the place of Inglishe
men, the Castell stanetinge in the most dangerous
place of all Munster.

Besids, ther is a band of soldiers, which a base
phello, O'DODALL, hath in Yoholl, which duth cost
the Queen twelve hundred pound a yeare, and hath
not ten good men in it; but our porest people
muster and serve hyme for threepence a day, and
the rest of his soldiers do nothing but spoyle the
country, and drive away our best tenants.

If the Queen be over rich, it may bee mayn-
tayned; but I will, att three days' warninge, rayse

her

her a better bande, and arme it better tenfold, and better men, whensoever shee shall need it. And, in the mean tyme, it may ether be imployed in the North, or discharged ; for ther is in Munster, besids, a band of horse, and another of foot, which is more than needeth. In this, if yow pleas to move it, yow may save her Majestye so mich in her coffers. For the rest I will send my man to attend yow, although I care not ether for life or lands ; but it will be no small weakninge to the Queen in thos parts, and no small cumfort to the ill-affected Irishe, to have the Inglishe inhabitants driven out of the country, which are yet stronge enough to master the rest, without her charge.

Yours, to do yow service,

W. RALEGH.

VIII

SIR,

I PRAY send me the news of Ireland. I
hear that there are three thousand of the BURGKS
in arms, and young ODONELL and the sons of
SHANE ONEALE. I wrote in a letter of Mr.
KILLEGREEW'S, ten days past, a prophesye of this
rebellion, which when the Queen read, she made a
scorn at my conceat; but yow shall find it but a
shoure of a farther tempest. If yow please to sent
me word of what yow hear, I will be laught at
again in my opinion touching the same, and be
bold to write yow my farther suspicion. Your
cousen, the dotinge Deputy, hath dispeopled me;
of which I have written to your father already. It
is a sign how my disgraces have past the seas, and
have

have been highly commended to that wise Governour, who hath used me accordingly. So I leve to trouble yow at this time, being become like a fish cast on dry land, gasping for breath, with lame leggs and lamer loonges. Your's, for the little while I shall desire to do yow service,

W. RALEGH.

To the right honorable, Sir ROBERT CICILL, *Knight, of
Her Majestie's most honorable Privy Councell.*

SIR,

I AM very sorry for MR. WILKENSON and the
rest, that I here ar lost in the River of Burdens;
but for my part I was resolved of the success before-
hand, and so miche I told WILLKENSON before his
departure. Of this Irish combinaction Her Majestye shall find it remembred to her sealf not
longe since; but the Troien Southsayer cast his
spear against the wooden horse, but not belevede
I did also presume to speake somewhat how to
prevent this purpose; and I thinck it not over
hard to be yet donn; and if I had by any chance
bynn acquaynted with the Lord BURGH's instructions, I would have putt you in mynde to have
woonne the Earle of Argile rather then all the rest
of Skotland; for by hyme this fier must be only

maintained

maintained in Ulstell. But for me to speake of the one or the other, I knowe my labors are prejudicate, and I cannot hereafter deserve ether thancks or acceptance. Less then that number men apoynted, I tacke it, will serve the turn, if the garrisons be placed aright to impeach the assemblies, and sume smale pineses ordered to lye between CANTIRRS and ODONELLS Country; but herein the order and the tyme hath most powere. Ther be also others in Irland that lye in waite, not suspected; which I most feare, and others most able and fitt to make them neglected and discoraged : which smale matters would have hartned to great purpose, as the tyme will better wittness. I had bynn able my sealf to have raysed to or three bands of Inglishe well armed, till I was driven to relinquishe and recale my people; of which the loss shall not be alone to mee, howsoever I am tumbled down the hill by every practize.

We ar so busyed and dandled in thes French warrs, which are endless, as we forgett the defens next the hart. Her Majesty hath good cause to

remember

remember that a million hath bynn spent in Irland not many yeares since. A better kingdome might have bynn purchased att a less prize, and that same defended with as many pence, if good order had bynn taken. But the question now may be, whether for so great expence the estate be not less asured then ever? If Her Majestye conseder it aright, she shall fynde it no small dishonor to be vexed with so beggerly a nacion, that have neather armes nor fortificasion; but that acursed kingdome hath always bynn but as a trafique, for which Her Majestye hath paid both fraight and costume, and others receved the marchandize; and other then such shall it never be. The Kinge of Spayne seeketh not Irlande for Irlande, but havinge raysed up troops of beggers in our backs, shall be able to inforce us to cast our eyes over our shoulders, while thos before us strike us on the braynes. We have also knowne the levell of his subversion; but destiney is stronger than councell; and good advice, ether neglected or weakly executed, hath tought our enemis to arme thos parts which before

lay

lay bare to the sworde. Prevention is the doughter of Intelligence, which cannot be borne without a mother; and the good wooman hath so many patrons, as the one referreth her cherishinge to another's trust, and in the meanwhile shee liveth baren and frutles.

Sir, thes poore Countris yeild no newse. I here of a frigott that taketh up fishermen for pilatts in the West. I am my sealf here at Sherburne, in my fortun's folde. Wherever I be, and while I am, yow shall cummande me. I thinck I shall need your furder favor for the litle parke, for Law and Conscience is not sufficient in thes days to upholde me. Every foole knoweth that hatreds are the cinders of affection, and therfore to make me a sacrifize shall be thanksworthye. Sir, I pray remember my duty to my Lord Admirall, and to your father, if it please yow.

From Sherburne, this 10th of May [1593].

Your's most asured to do yow service,

W. RALEGH.

I am the worse for the Bath, and not the better.

X

To the Lord Treasurer BURGHLEY.

MY HONORABLE GOOD LORD,

By reason of your Lordship's letters and the rest of the Lords of Her Majesties Privie Councell, written to the Lord Deputie and Councell of Ireland, for a restraint of transportacion of Pipe-staves out of that Realme to the Islands, we have a great quantitie of barrell and hogshead bords alreadie cutt and made which, for want of venting and expending, will rott uppon the ground, if we maie not receave some order for their utterance. Besides, we must be forced to draw home a great number of able men from thence which are appointed to serve Her Majestie with their weapons uppon anie occasion, which will prove to be a great weakening of the province of Munster.

Wherefore, if it please your Lordship,—for the

keeping

keeping and enterteyning of theis men in worke, which otherwise cannot live there; and for venting of this commoditie, which must needs perish if longer staie be made of them there,—to write to the Lord Deputie and Councell, that, according to your Lordship's meaning signified in your former letters, we maie be licensed to transport from thence into England such barrell and hogshead bords as we have made, and maie be sparde out of our own woods; the rather, because those of the west countrie here have great want of this caske, we will putt in such bords to her Majesty's use, before th' officers of the ports where they are to be laden, as are required in your Lordship's said letters, for th' assured transporting thereof into England and to no other place. And so I most humblie take my leave. From Dirrham House, the xvth of June, 1593.

Your Lordship's for ever to be cummanded,

W. RALEGH.

For the bringinge of caske into Ireland, I hope wee

wee shall rather deserve thankes, then that wee shall need to make any great sutes for it. Yet, so mich it hath pleased the Deputye to malline my particuler, as I know, without your Lordshipp's heulpe, yeven so mich will hardly be afforded. I do humblie desire your Lordship to favor mee so mich as to writ your Lordship's own letteres unto hyme that I may receve justice at his hands; and, acknowledging my sealf only bound and susteyned by your Lordship's goodnes, I wishe your Lordship eternall health, and humblie take my leave.

XI

To the right honorable Sir ROBERT CECIL, *Knight, one of
her Majesties most honorable Privie Councell.*

SIR,

You know our long suite to the Lords of Her
Majesties Privie Councell for the continuance of
transportation of Pipestaves out of Ireland to the
Islandes, according to Her Majesties graunt by Her
Letters Patents under the Great Seale.   Master
PINE, as I understand, is now at Court to sollicite
your Honnor and the rest, in our behalfe, for a
dissolucion of the restraint procured by the Lord
Deputie's letters, upon his supposicion of some
enormities and surmised inconveniences which
thereby will need ensue.

I beeseech your Honnor to fauvor our proceedings therein, and to assist us, as much as you maie,
for the obteyning of our suite ; and if you please to

acquaint

acquaint my Lord Admiral with my poore request, I doubt not but his Lordship will farther so honest a mocion.

If their Lordships would be pleased thoroughlie to consider the state of the cause, and have patience to peruse the contents of our demaund (which Master PINE will shew your Honnor, in all points, according to the truth), they wold assuredlie allow of our trade to the Islands, and conceave better of those which undertake the same.   And so I humblie take my leave.

From Gillingham Forrest, the 27th of August, 1593.

Your Honor's humblie att cummandment,

W. RALEGH.

Sir, The Indian falcon is sike of the buckworme ; and therfore, if yow wilbe so bountefull to geve another falcon, I will provide yow a roning geldinge.

XII

To the right honorable Sir ROBERT CECILL, *Knight, one of her Majesties most honorable Privy Councell.*

SIR,

THIS honorable gentleman, the Lord BARRY, one that is well affected to her Majesty and her Estate, is in humble suite to her Majesty, and hath entreated my letter to your Honnor that such fine or benefitt as FLORENCE MACCARTY hath by graunt obteined from her Majesty, by reason of his former offence in Ireland (which is well knowen to your Honnor), may be again revoked and remitted.

And if my opinion herein maybe reguarded, I thinke that his pardon which her Highnes graunted him hath wrought his true affection, and his entire disposicion to honnor and serve her Maiesty with such unfeined obedience as can be required; and therfore not fitt to be discountenanced by FLORENCE MACCARTY, [he] being a man reconciled to the

Pope,

Pope, daungerous to the present State, beloved of such as seeke the ruine of the Realme his native cuntrie, and not worthie to bee relieved by her Maiesties goodnes. He maie for a time dissemble, and in revealing his poverty, by occasion of his imprisonment in the Tower, protest that obedience which he ought to performe : but he is not to be trusted. His alliance and friends in Ireland are great and manie, and he wanteth nothing but mony to execute his practices, whereunto the Pope hath animated him.

This noble gentleman hath, to my knowledg, a long time lived civilly and conformablie to all her Majesties directions and commandments, and hath not deserved theis troubles and discontentments. I praie you so much to favour him by yourself, or by the meanes of my honorable good Lord, your father, that hee maie bee discharged of this demaund ; and I will reckon it amongst the rest of your favours. And so I humblie take my leave.

From th' assises at Dorchester, the 4th of March, 1593. Your Honor's humblie att cummandment,

W. RALEGH.

XIII

To the right honorable Sir ROBERT CECILL, *Knight, of
her Majesties most honorable Privey Councell.*

SIR,

FROM this desolate place I have little matter ;
from myself, less hope ; and therefore I thinke the
shorter the discourse, the better wellcum.

I receved from Lyme,—a port town in this shire,
—by a smale barke lately arived, that there ar
lately many French shipps imbargoed in Spayne,
and of good burden and very serviceable ; notwithstanding that the same went by pasport and
asurance from Spayne. And all the marriners
likewise imprested ; and that ther ar a fleet ether
gone or goinge of sixtye saile, as the saye, for
Irlande. It seemeth asuredly that the preparations
ar great, and do dayly increase.

If your Honors conceave therof aright, or looke
into

into the nirest mischeif, wee shall do the better. Butt I feare, by your favors, ther is somewhat more in the enemys intent then is supposed. Wee that have mich ado to gett bread to eat have the less to care for, unless mich lost labor and love awake us that ar also thanckles busied in things ether beyound our capasates or cares.

What becumes of Guiana I miche desire to here, —whether it pass for a history or a fable. I here Mr. DUDLEY and others ar sendinge thither; if it be so, farewell all good from thence. For although my sealf,—like a cockscome,—did rather preferr the future, in respect of others; and rather sought to wine the kings to her Majesties service then to sack them, I know what others will do, when thos kings shall cum simpely into their hands. If it may pleas yow to acquaynt my Lord Admirall therwith, lett it then succeed as it wille.

If my Lord will have a fyne pinnes sent to the coast of Spayne, to vew what is dunn, I thinke for a matter of £40 or £50 I can gett one that shall do service.

Sir,

Sir, for conclusion, I will only say this mich,—take good heed least you be not to slow. Expedition in a little is better than mich, to late. Butt yow, ministers of dispatch, ar not plentifull. Neather is it every man's occupation. God send yow all honor and health. I will wishe yow both, and be reddy ever to do yow service,

W. RALEGH.

From Sherborne, the 10th of November [1595].

XIV

To the right honorable Sir ROBERTE CECILL, *Knighte,*
Counceller in her Highnes' Prevye Councelles.

THESE maye be to seignifye unto your Honor that
the Archebishopp of Cashell, a man whome, I
thincke, my Lord Treasourer hathe lytell cause to
favor, hathe of late delte verye badlye with me,
contrarye to all faythe and promysse, touchinge
diverse of my Irishe leases and lands; whoes
discortysies I wold gladlye mete withall. And doe
fynde noe better meanes in releffe of my self,
fartheraunce of relygyon, and comforte of all myne
Inglyshe tenants and frendes, then in preferrynge
some other of better sorte to the bishoppricke of
Lesmore and Waterforde, whereof the Archebishop
hathe but a comende, and hathe, besydes, twoe or
three other bishoprickes.

My desire is that you wilbe pleased to be a
meane

meane to prefer unto the same bishopricke of Lesmore and Waterford my verye good frend Master HUGHE BROUGHTON, a man well knowen to my Lorde his Grace of Caunterburye, my Lorde Treasorer, and all the lerned docters and scollers of Englande; and a man unto whome I wishe moche goode; besechinge you to have some conference with my cosen GORINGE aboughte he same—wherein the said Master BROUTON is able to do moche good and be a greate comforte to all our Inglishe nation thereaboughtes, and encrease of relygyon. And the gentellman hymself wilbe verye thanckefull unto you for anye favor shewed unto hym, whome I leave to your good rememberance, and your self to God. This third of Maye, 1596.

Your Honor's to do yow service,

W. RALEGH.

To Sir Robert Cycill.

XV

To the right honorable Sir ROBERT CECIL, *Knight,*
Principall Secretory to her Maiestie.

SIR,

IT can be no disgrace if it weare knowen that
the killinge of a rebel weare practised; for you see
that the lives of anoynted Princes are daylye sought,
and we have always in Ireland geven head money
for the killinge of rebels, who ar evermore proclaymed at a price. So was the Earle of
DESMONDE, and so have all rebels been practised
agaynst. Notwithstandinge, I have written this
enclosed to STAFFORD, who only recommended
that knave to me upon his credit. Butt, for your
sealf, you ar not to be touched in the matter. And
for me, I am more sorrye for beinge deceaved than
for beinge declared in the practise.

Your Lordship's, ever to do you service,

W. RALEGH.

He hathe nothinge under my hand butt a passport.

XVI

To the right honorabell Sir ROBERT CECYLL, *Knight,*
Principall Secritory to her Majestye.

SIR,

    I BESEICH you to signefye Her Majesties pleasure to my Lord Deputye of Irland—because his Lordship is ready to depart—concerning this gentelman, on whom Her Majestye hathe bestowed POORE'S companye.

          Your Honor's to do you service,

                    W. RALEGH.

XVII

I WROTE unto yow the 26 of this present what I
received from certayne Skottishe marchants. It is
now manefest that bothe thos advertisements ar
trew, for thos three pinneses which brought in the
great prize att Plymouth of 900 chests of suger were
chased by the Spanish fleet, seven dayes before
their arivall; and they arived on Tuesday last, the
second of this moneath, and weare therfore chased
of the mouth of the Channell, which was about the
25 of August, and so must needs be in Ireland or
perished; from whence it seemeth yow canot hear
by reason of this esterly winde.

Thos of Munster had some warninge of ther
being on the coast, for one Captayne LOVE or
Capt. LANE, being on the Irishe coast, forsooke
his shipp, and went into a bote and tooke horse
uppon

uppon the shore, and gave warninge to the next adjoyninge about the coast of Dungarvan, between Yoholl and Waterforde. From there he tooke his shipp agayne and arived att Plymoth. Thes pinneses tolde 60 sayle. A Fleming also, cuming from Lysbone, confirmeth the former intelligence, and addeth therunto, either out of conjecture, or knowledge, or fame, affirming that the soldiers ar 6,000; that they have twelvemoneths pay, and like vittell, beforehande; that he saw many with chaynes of golde; and that generally the army was very brave, and well provided of all things; that certayne cannons were imbarked in some gallions, with all other things answerabell.

Sir, I beseich to acquaynt my Lord Admirrall herewith, and that yow will vouchsaif to excuse me for not writing to his L, knowing that yow are of one mind and fortune, of one love and on indevor for Her Majesties service.

Yours ever as your sarvent,

W. RALEGH.

Shirb, the 27 of Sept., 1601.

XVIII

To the right honorabell Sir ROBERT CECYLL, *Knight, Principall Secritorye, &c.*

SIR,

If I cum not to late, I would be an humbell sutor unto yow for a cumpany in Irland for a gentelman, Mr. STUCKLY, who hath served with good reputation bothe by sea and lande. Hee was wounded with Sir RICHARD GRENVILE in the *Revendge*, and hath since served longue in Irland and elcewhere. For the rest, I will not trobell yow, but I will hope for your favor towards hyme, and rest your Honors to do yow service,

W. RALEGH.

Sherburn, this 13 of October, 1601.

This bearer hath brought an Inglishman which came in the Spanish fleet. Hee will tell yow that they imbarked 4,000 men, but want ij great shipps and almost a 2,000 of their men. They ar riche in mony.

mony. The cummanders have brought their wives and children, which proveth that they mean to abide it, and make us a warr ther. They look for great supplies. They have broken down the wall, man's hight. They have intrenched without the towne; out of which they have bynn beaten twise in a day by Captain FLOWRE. The Inglishe serve with invincibell currage agaynst them. Many Spanierds ar alreddy taken. They have too carvells uppon the entrance. The Deputy is not yet cum to beseige them, but will shortly. DIEGO BROCHERO is admirall; SEBURO, vice-admirall. BROCHERO is thot dead. They had 6 great shipps of 900 toon, and on of 1,300; all mand, for the most, with strangers. The most of the shipps ar gone. The rest tarry yet.

I had thought that this bearer had been STUCKLY, which made me write as I did. Butt he is still in Irlande, and therfore I do not miche desire anything in his behalf.

Your's ever to do yow service,

Sherburn, this Wensday night. W. R.

XIX

To the right honorabell Sir ROBERT CECYLL, *Knighte, Principall Secritorye, &c.*

SIR,

I AM of oppinion that ether Kynsale was not the place purposed to be undertaken, or elce FLORENCE [MACCARTHY] was the cause therof, for the port bordereth his country. The towne is of small reseate, mastered by hills, and cumpassed with a weake wall. Butt wher as I herd that the Deputy and Presedent have written that they will make a short work of it, I am not altogether of that minde, and yet I do not thinck that Spayne will supply them in hast. Neather will thos Spanierds alreddy ther finde such a party as they hoped,— which may be some cause of thos governours' hopes. Butt, after a few dayes, yow shall here more; for, if the country stand sounde, then the

warr

warr wilbe the easier. Butt sure I am if thes Spanierds had cum in the begining of the warrs, the kingdome had bynn once lost. Yow shall finde, I warrant yow, that TIRRONE will bestire hyme sealf in the north, and every rebell in his quarter. For this is the last of all hopes.

For MEERES, I thinck by this tyme yow finde the strenght of his villanous spirrite, and yet a more notorious cowardly brute never lived. Butt if hee do not submitt hyme sealfe, hee will triumph that hee hath resisted mee and my greatest frinds. All which I leve to your favorabell care, and rest your ever most faythfull, to do yow service,

W. RALEGH.

My wife sayes that yow came hither in an unseasonabell tyme, and had no leasure to looke abrode ; and that every day this place amends, and London, to her, groes worss and worss. I have sent away her Majestie's letters and your Honor's with all dillegence ; not doubting butt the soldiers, butt first apoynted and thes, shalbe reddy. My

deputes

deputes have written to mee that they will arme the first 50 men.   What they will do for thes, I know not

Endorsed : "*Sir Walter Raleigh to my Master.   Without date ;*" and in another hand, " *Oct.* 1601."

XX

Testamentary Note written by Sir Walter Ralegh on the night before his execution, November, 1618.

A Copy of the note written by Sir Walter Rawley, in his owne hand, which hee gave me for discharge of his conscience, &c.
Endorsement of Sir Thomas Wilson, Keeper of the Tower.

THERE is a lease of certaine parcells of land, claymed by one JOHN MEERE, near Sherborne Castle. MEERE clayming it by a grant of myne to one Captain THOMAS CAUFEILDE, I do protest before God I never made any lease or grant to CAUFEILDE of that land.

There is a lease in controversy betweene the Lord BOYLE and one HENRY PINE, of the Castle and lands of Mogile, in the county of Corck in Ireland; and although I did write something at my going from Ireland towards Guiana to the prejudice of PINE's lease, yet since that time better bethinking myself,

myself, I desire that the opinion which I gave of PINE'S lease may be no evidence in law against PINE, but that it may be left to other prooffs on both sydes.

I desire that my wife, if shee enjoy her goods, may have consideration of CHRISTOPHER HAMON'S wyfe. That my wife do in any case, according to her ability, releive Mr. JOHN TALBOT'S wife, who, I feare me,—her sonn being deade,—will otherwise perish.

Sir LEWIS STUKELEY sold all the tobacco at Plimouth of which, for the most part of it, I gave him a fift part of it, as also a role for my Lord Admirall and a role for himself. He had also tenn peeces of mee the Sonday that wee tooke boate, which he pretended to borrow to send his men into the country, which notwithstanding hee sent downe the river to joyne with Mr. HARBERT I desire that hee may give his account for the tobacco.

W. RALEGH.

APPENDIX

APPENDIX

Official Report of Proceedings at Smerwicke:
Women hanged and Two Men mutilated.

STATE PAPERS—IRELAND, 1580, NOVEMBER.

VOL. 78. NO. 27.

The vi[th] of this Monethe my Lorde lieinge in
Campe betwene Dingley and Smerwicke newes
came to his Honor of the arrivall of S[r] Will'm
Winter in the haven of Smerwick withe the
Revendge, the Swifte Sure, the Tyger & the
Merlyon and other Shippes of her Ma[ty], & also
of three barques fraughted from Lymerick and
Corke w[th] victuells vppon w[ch] advertism[t] his Lo:
on the morrowe after m'ched towardes the fortes
and comynge w[th]in vewe thereof the Spanyardes
dischardged a great peece at a trope of Horsmen
attendinge his honnor, at w[ch] tyme the M[r] of
Thordnnce verie narowlie escaped. And the
vovewarde marchinge of my Lo: w[th] a smale Company drewe nere w[th]in dawnger of shott where-
vppon

vppon xxx^tie of the forte issued forthe and did
skirmishe wth o^r men that after none, and theare
great ordn'nce and certayne muskett^rs lienge at
rest in certayne trenches dischardged at vs as
faste as might be and the Shippes wth theire
ordn'nce at the fortes duringe wch tyme my͡ Lo:
in psone Mr Zouche & other attendinge hime
tooke vewe of the fortes, and came w^thin vj score
paces of the Rampier there was dischardged out
of the fortes above vi^c shott that after none greate
and smale and no man towched on o^r syde (god
be praysed) savinge that a Bullett from the forte
after grazinge towched Cap^ten Zouche on the legg
and brake noe skine, and of the ennymyes, three
slayne of there best Showldiers. That night two
peeces of Ordyn'nce was landed and movnted and
a trench made by the Showldyors and marryners
and on the morrowe playde all the daye at the
fortes and they likewise at vs besydes skyrmishinge
betwene them and o^r Showldiers and no man of
o^r pte hurte but of them ix of there chefest
souldiors and one Cap^ten were slayne wth two
shott of o^r Ordyn'nce & the night after wth a
Rowlinge Trenche we came w^thin vj score of the
forte, and on the morrowe after certaine of o^r shott
were placed in the same trenche where Mr Cheike
showing himselfe was shott in the head wth a

bullett

bullett & is in great daunger of deathe. At o^r firste comynge they advaunced iiij Ensignes & the Poopes banner in the middest of thinn'r forte wch on the viijth daye they tooke downe and did set vpp two other, one all white and another all black wch was for a token devised betwene Therle and then the meaning wherof was that if they fownde them selves weeke and vnable to ķepe the fortes then Therle and John p'mysed to be on the movntaynes by wth M^{l}M^{l}M^l mene, and vppon sight therof come downe wth there forces & Remove o^r seidge, but in conclusion they never shewed their selves vppon wch the morrowe after the black flagg was taken downe and the white lefte standinge wch they waved towards us makinge an offer to pley. Vpon intelligence wherof geven to my Lo: his honnor sent Capt. Zouch and Capt. Mackworthe vnto them by whome they sente from the forte one of there cheifest menne called Alexander there Campe M^r and one Plunckett borne nere to Drogheda, and after some conference had by my Lo: wth them, his honnor retorned them backe willing them to sende their cheifest Cap^{tens} wch they did accordingly who comynge to his Lo: after some discourses of Faulke offred to yeeld vpp the ffortes, Soe as they might be licensed to depte wth Bag and baggadge

w^{ch}

wch my Lo: did not graune vnto them, Wheruppon after his Lo: had declared vnto them that vnlesse they wolde simplie yeelde them selves wthout condic'on his Lo: wolde p'ceede to the assavlte and so they were sent backe to there Collonell where after they had remayned some while in consultac'on the Collonell and Cap^{tens} came forth and yelded to my Lo: demaundes and lefte pledges to yealde vp the fforte the next morninge and brought wth them Sr James ffitzgarrett who was taken by the Seneshall and given to them by Therle to be Ransomed at M^{li}.

The morrowe after beinge the ixth of this monethe the ffortes were yeelded all the Irishmen and women hanged, and iiij^c and vpwardes of Italyans, Spanyardes, Byskins and others put to the sworde. The Collonell, Captⁿ Secretarie Camp M^r and others of the best sorte saved to the number of xx^{tie} psones and doctor Saund . . . chief man an Englishman Plunckett a ffrayer and others kept in store to be executed after examynac'on had of them.

It is confessed that v^{ml} more are loked for daylie to be sente from the Pope and the Kinge of Spayne to lande here.

There was fownde in the ffortes good store of mony and a great quantitie of bisquett, Bacon,

oyle,

oyle, ffishe, Rise, Beanes, peas, Barley beinge by computac'on victuelles for there Company for halfe a yeare. There was also fownde Armor, morrions callyvers, mvsketts, pykes, swordes, fflasqes harquebusses of croke, powder, shott, barrells of bulletts and other kinde of furniture to serve iiij^{ml} and sondry tooles for mene of all occupac'ons.

My Lo: after the Rasinge of the ffortes entendeth to repayre to Dingley, and there to fortefie and leave Capten Zouche with ccccl^{ti} mene and soe to come homewardes throughe Connought as it is Reported.

This daye was Exec'ted an Englishman who served Doctor Sawnders, one Plunckett of whome before is wryten and an Irishe Preste theire armes and Legges were Broken and hanged vppon a Gallowes vppon the Wall of the fforte.

Endorsed : *" To the right honorable S^r ffrauncs Walsingham Knight principall Secretary to her......and of her most honorable......counsell yeue these hast."*

Queen Elizabeth's Letters about the Affair at Smerwick

This was writtyn in Roman hand by her Ma. on the top of the Lre. } The mightie hand of the Al-mightiest power hathe showed manifest the force of his strengthe in the weakenes of feeblest sexe and mynds this yere to make men asshamed ever hereafter to disdaine vs, in wch Action I joye that you have bin chose the Instrument of his glory wch I meane to give you no cause to forthincke. Your loving Soveraygne,

ELIZABETH R.

By the Queene.

Trusty, &c. As the most happie successe youe haue latly had against certaine invad^{rs} sent by the Pope contayned in yor l'res brought vnto vs by ou^r seruant Denny doth incomparably shew the great-nes of god's loue & fauo^r towards vs; so yor care & paine in following of the same and courage in execuc'on thereof, deserueth great thancks & comen-dac'ons at our hands. Wherein youe haue answered

by

by effects ye good opinion we conceaued of yor sufficiency at the tyme of our choise made of youe, to supply the place youe do now hold : not doubting but that hereafter there will appeare greater fruits of yor valeur by reducing the deseased state of ye realme to such conformity as god may be better serued, we obayed and this our Realme not burthened wth charges as of late yeres it hath ben : wherein assure yor self youe shall not lack ou^r good countenance and fauo^r in such measure as neyther enny nor practise shalbe able to preuayle against youe, & therefore vppon this assurance youe may proceede wth the more comfort in the charg comitted vnto youe. In this late enterprise performed by youe so greatly to ou^r lyking we could haue wished that the p^{r}ncipal persons of the said invad^{rs} to whome youe haue p'mised grace wch we will see performed, had ben reserued for vs, to haue extended towards them eyther Justice or mercy, as to vs should have ben founde best, ffor y^t it seemeth to vs most agreable to reason that a principall should receaue punishment before an accessary, wch would haue serued for a terro^r to such as may be hereafter drawen to be executioners of so wicked an enterprise when they should heare that aswell the heads as the inferio^{rs} had receaued punishment according to theire demerits. Vppon the great

good

good report youe haue giuen vnto vs of such
Captaines & soldiers as in this enterpise did assist
youe for theire great forwardnes & courage shewed
in performing this so acceptable a service to vs we
would haue youe let them vnderstand in how
thanckfull part we accept the same, and so much
the rather for y^t we haue ben informed what great
pennury they haue sustayned in our seruice there
not only for want of necessary victuell, but also in
respect of the badnes and vnseruiceablenes of such
scarcety as they had.　Wherein as we to our great
greefe howlding nothing so deear as the pr'seruac'on
of the healthe and lyves of the subjects thinck our-
self very ill s'rved by such inferior mynisters to
whome the charg thereof hath ben comitted, so
you may let them vnderstande y^t we will see y^t
better order be taken hereafter aswell in that as in
all oth^r things requisite for theire better comfort
and encouragement & for the advancement of our
s'ruice.

　　Endorsed : " 12° *Decemb.* 1580 *at Westm^r.　Minute from
the Queenes Ma^{te} to the L. Gray L. depute of Ireland."*
Entered.

————

Right trustye &c.　Whereas we have ben in-
fourmed that certen reports haue ben caryed ou'r

vnto

vnto yo, that you should be out of o^r grace and fauor, wherwth we heare you are greatly greeved and discompforted, we haue thought good to let you vnderstand that though in very deede we haue conceaued some mislike of the continuance of o^r great chardgs in that realme and for that things weare not so carefully looked vnto and husbanded for our most proffit, as y^t seemid vnto vs they might haue ben but rather that there was some more regarde had to ye gratefyeing of ye Captens and Souldio^{rs} especyally by contyneweing dyvines in pension vppon no great cavse of desert by servyce as also couered vnnecessary offycers then of easing of o^r chardgs, and that so great numbers, as the garrison did of late ryse vnto, weare continued longer in paye then the necessitye of o^r s'ruice (weying the burthen of th' excessyve chardgs we did therby susteyne,) did require, yet the same mislike did not proceede so farr to make vs forgett the great good s'rvics you haue don vs many wayes but cheefely in the late exployt you did against the straingers that had invaded ye realme, wch next to gods dyvyne providence we must needes acknowledge as the second meanes wherbye the whole land was pres'rued from the hazard and danger wch otherwyes y^t was likely to haue fallen into, for the wch as we do carye a thanckfull remembraunce

towards

towards you, so do we still retayne that good
opinion we haue alwayes conceyuid of yor syncere
good will and deuoc'on to the furtheraunce of o^r
s'ruice accompanyed wth no lesse fidelitye and
sufficiencye eny waye to pfourme the same.
Wherfore we wishe you not to be any way greeued
or discouraged thorough any such sinister reports
as may be made vnto you of o^r meaning towards
you but rather to proceede on cherefully to do yor
best indevo^r in ye well executing of ye chardge
comitted vnto you, as we ar in good hope by yor
meanes and carefull trauell that realme shalbe
shortlye reduced to such a setled and peaceable
estate of gou'rnement as both o^r chardges shalbe
hereafter spared and the people conteynid wthin
the bounds of due obedyence towards vs, for the
bringinge wherof to passe according to such order
and direction as you shall receaue from vs iu that
behalf, you shall not want o^r best fauo^r helpe and
counten'nce, as ap'teyneth to a man of yor qualitye
& good des'rte that occupyeth that place in o^r
s'ruice tha you do and of whom we haue conceaued
so good an opinion & liking.

Endorsed : " *From hir Matie to the L: Deputie.*" Entred.

III

III

Sir Walter Ralegh's Reckonings

STATE PAPERS—IRELAND, 1583, JAN.-FEB.

BUNDLE 99.

THE reconynge or Accompte of Walter Rawleic gent, Captaine of Cth ffootemen for such somes of moneie as by her Matie is growne dewe vnto him and the Bande vnder his Leadinge, viz. :—

ffirst for the wages of him selfe at iiij^s p diem a pete captaine ij^s p diem, iiij^or officers xij^d the peice & C^th ffootemen at viij^d

the peice p diem for iiij daies begin' xiij° Julii 1580 and ending the laste of Septem' following amount vnto vnto as by Warrnnte of the xx^th of Decemb'r 1580 appeareth.

cccvj^l xiij^s iiij^d [Ex]

And for his saide wagies of iiij^s p diem a petecaptaine ij^s iiij^or officers xij^d the peice and C^th ffootemen at viij^d the peice p diem for ciiij ij^j daies begin' p^mo Apr'lis 1582 and ending vltmio Septem' following as by Warrnnte xx^mo Novemb'r 1582 app'eth.

dccj^l x^s [Ex]

Also for the wagies of xij horsemen at ix^d the peice p diem for ciiij iij daies begin' p^mo Apr'lis 1582 & ending the last of Septemb'r followinge as by Warrnnte xx^mo Novemb'r 1582 app'eth.

xx iiij iiij^l ij^l vij^s [Ex]

And lastlie he is allowed odd pence for victualling of his footeband and horsemen aforesayde viz :—cvj allowan' for his footebande at j^d per everie allowance p diem for ccccxlv daies begin' xiij° Julii 1580 and endinge the last of Septemb'r 1582 ciiij xvij^l x^s x^d ster. and xij allowances for the saide horsem' at v^d per everie allowance p diem for ccxlij daies begin' p^mo ffebruar' 1580 and ending the last of Septemb'r afforesayd—lxiij^l x^s vj^d ex'ster. Amounting in all by Concordatu' of the xxvij^th of Decemb'r 1582 To cclx^l xvj^d ster. fac' irish.

cccxlvj^l xv^s j^d [Ex]

mccccxxvij^l v^s v^d ob' whereof.

(margin notes: sic; The sayde Capt^a Walter Rawleic hathe dewc.)

	dcxiij^l xv^s ij^d q^i	dcccxxiij^l ix^s iij^d q^i
Cheques contayned in the laste Warrnte for ffootemen		
Checked of Thodd pence	lxxvj^l x^s viij^d	
Prestes by Sr Henrie Walloppe Knighte Tre'r at Warres by certyfic' of Michaell Ketlewell	xxxvlij^l xviij^s iij^d ob' q^i	
Victnells certyfied by Thom's Mighte cxxx^l xiiij^s xj^d by Jo. Thickpennye lxx^l ix^s v^d and by Ja. Brunklowe xl^l v^s vj^d ob' In all ccxlj^l ix^s j^d ob' wch is charged ster. for that he is allowed odd pence for victuellinge moneie and maketh irishe	xxxviij^l iij^s iij^d q^i	
Munycons certyfied by the M^r of the Ordynnce	cccxxj^l xviij^s x^d	
Beoves of the Marshall in the Campe xxviij daies at xij^d the peice	cxxij^l iij^s j^d	
The clerke of the Checques Deputie	xvij^l ij^s	
Will'm Puckring S^rgeon	lxj^s x^d	
The Citizens of Lymricke by bill xix° Novemb'r 1580 vij^l v^s ster. and bill of the xj^th of Aprill 1582 signed by Michaell Buttler his Liuetennte viij^s iiij^d 'sterling. In all sterling— vij^l xiij^s iiij^d making irish	xlij^s x^d	x^l iiij^s v^d q^i
Thinhabitnnts of Clonmell by bill of the xth of Juñe 1582 signed by Michaell Buttler xlv^s iiij^d ster' fac' ir'		lx^l v^d q^i
Thinhabitnnts of Killmallocke by bill xxvij^th Novemb'r 1580— xxx^s ster' making irish		xl^s
Him selfe		dcccij^l xix^s viij^d ob' q^i ir' making sterling dcij^l iiij^s ix^d ob'
M^d &c.		
Endorsed Captain Rawleies first Reconynge.		

And so remayneth dewe To

STATE PAPERS—IRELAND, 1583, JAN.-FEB.

BUNDLE 99—(continued).

dclij xˢ xjᵈ obᵒ diˢ qˢ whereof.

ffor the wageis of hym selfe at iiijˢ p diem, a pete-captaine ijˢ iiijᵒʳ officers xijᵈ the peice and Cth ffootemen at viijᵈ the peice exr p diem for cxliij daies begin' the first of October 1582 and ending the xxᵗʰ of ffebruar' next following wᵗʰ daie they weare dischardged as by Warrnnte of the last of ffebruar' 1582 app'eth	dxlviijˡ iijˢ iiijᵈ (exr)
Also for the wagies of xij horsemen at ixᵈ the peice p diem ffor the tyme afforesayd as by Warrnnte vltio ffebruar' 1582 app'eth	lxiiijˡ vijˢ (exr)
And for the wagies of Ruben Senton Victualle' vnto the sayd bande in respecte of Wastes and Losses sustayned by yssuing of victuells to the sayde companie for the sayde cxliij daies begin' and ending as afforesaide at viijᵈ p diem by Warrnnte of the Last of ffebruar' 1582	iiijˡ xvˢ iiijᵈ (exr)
Also for thallowance of odd pence for victualling of his sayde bande viz :—cvj allowances at jᵈ ster' the peice p diem for cxliij daies begin' p'mo Octob'r 1581 and ending the xxᵗʰ of ffebruarie ffollowing amounting to by Concordatu' vlti'o ffebruar' 1582 lxiiijˡ iijˢ ijᵈ obᵒ qˢ sterlinge making irish	xx iiij iiijˡ iiijˢ iiijᵈ obᵒ diˢ qˢ (exr)
And lastlie for Oate and victualling moneie for the saide xij horsemen at vᵈ qˢ ster. the peice p diem for cxliij daies begin' the first of October 1582 and ending the xxᵗʰ of ffebruar' next following amount' to as by Concordatu' of the sayde last of ffebruar' 1582 app'eth xxxvijˡ xˢ ixᵈ ster. fac' irish	lˡ xij (exr)

Dewe to him

		$cclvij^{li}$ xl^s vj^d di'		$\overset{xx}{ccccliiij^{li}}$ xv^s vj^d q'

	Checques contayned in the first Warrmnte of ffull paie	$xvij^{li}$ vj^s vj^d
	Checked also of thodd pence xl^s ix^d ob' q' ster' fac' irish	$liij^s$ v^d
Deducted for	Prestes by Sr Henry Walloppe Knighte Tre'r by certyficate of Michaell Ketlewell	$clxvij^{li}$ vj^s $viij^d$
	Victuells certefied by Thomas Mighte Victualler ccv^{li} $xviij^d$ and by James Brunklowe $lxxviij^s$ $iiij^d$ In all $ccviij^{li}$ xix^s x^d wth is chardged ster. for that he hath allowance of odd pence for victualling moneie & maketh irish	$cclxxviij^{li}$ $xiij^s$ j^d q'
	Munyc'ons certefyed by the M^r of Thordynnce	xxix^{li} xix^s x^d
	The Clerke of the checques deputie	$xxxiij^s$ $iiij^d$
	Will'm Pickringe Surgeon	$xxxiij^s$ $iiij^d$
	Thom's Holmes Soldioure by Tickett signed by Michaell Butler	ix^{li} xv^s v^d q'
And so rem' dewe To	Luieten' vij^{li} vj^s $iiij^d$ sterlinge making irish Richard Dickinson soldiour by Tickett signed by the sayde Luieten' $iiij^{li}$ iij^s vj^d ster' making irish	cxj^s $iiij^d$
	Him selfe	$ccxxxvij$ l $xvij^s$ di' q' ir' making sterlinge $clxxviij^l$ vij^s ix^d
	M^d &c.	
	Endorsed Captaine Rawleies seconde Reconynge.	

IV

Captain Ralegh's Pay

STATE PAPERS—IRELAND, 1582, FEB.

VOL. 89. No. 26.

Sr Henry Wallop to my L.

11 *feb.* 1581.

Ryght honorable, by a letter of S^r ffrauncs Wallsinghames of the first herof I perceve ther is 5000^{li} assygned for ye payment of the 700 last discharged, wherof by order ther is paide to Sr George Bowser 300^{li}, to Sr Nicholas Malbie 200^{li} and to Mr. Rawley 200^{li}.

My good L. my hope is that vpon the former certificats what mony more is requisite tobe had for the full paie of the three thousand and odd first discharged, and the great wants those yet in paie are in for lacke of mony and certaine debtts besydes due here to sondrie Parsons as by my particular lett^r appeereth that much the rather by yor L. good meanes money answerable to the necessities shalbe sent and therefore of that matter will no further troble yor L. being right sorie that I am so continually enforced thervnto for meny causes.

Yf

Yf her ma^tie^ might be drawen to make a full paie and then advaunce allwaies such a som'e as might serve for the garysons here (wch now are not great) for iij moneths, so as the soldio^r^ might eith^r^ have his moneths paie before hand, or paide him at the ende of everie monethe, in my symple opinion it wolde much advance the service, be profitable for hir ma^tie^ and avoid many inconveniencies.

Captn Barkeley is nowe discharged of his whole band, who I thinke will fall out quaid by reason he is continually victualled out of the store, and of the 800^li^ he had at one tyme off Pellysons agents in mony and wares as formerly I adu'rtised yor L: I gave no certificat that any such som'e was due to the said Captn, and therfore yor L. may staie the payment of the said Pollyson, oth'waies ye losse wilbe her ma^ties^.

I perceve that Pollysons agents both here and in Mounster have gotten and daylie do gett many billes into ther hands, thoughe I haue forewarned them that I will certifie none of them into England. I haue thought it also my duetie therof to certifie yor L. that they may not be paid in England, for yf they be, over many of o^r^ Captaines will fall out quaid, and I not able to helpe it, wch falleth owt nowe in the late Captn ffyrres, his reckoning, that by reason if billes certified into England that I am

not

not acquainted wth his dewe is not sufficient to paie his victualls, munition, and satisfie his company.

Yf all billes certified Mr Audito^r shalbe paid in England, the losse wilbe great to hir ma^{tie}, and my accompt much the more troblesome, wherfore I am most humbly to intreat yor L. that no paiement of any billes may be made but by me, or my assignement.

ffor Captⁿ Rawley, his owne request was of the 600 odde pounds due to him at Michaelmasse, that yf I had had y^t to have paid his agent here, the one halfe sholde have bene sent to his companie. Wherfore it shall do well he be paid no more vntill his company be satisfied and his accompt made, ffor not knowing nor having geven any direction ffor his paiement in England, vpon his discharge I sent his company 200^{li} into Mounster. Wherwth craving pardon of my co'tinuall over boldnes most humbly I take my Leave of yor L. praying Th' almyghtie longe to prosper yo^u.

Yo^r L. most bounden and at com'aundement,

H. WALLOP.

Dublin this xith of februarie 1581.

Endorsed : " *To the ryght honorable my very good L. the L. Burleigh.....gh Treasure' of England....these at the Courte.*

V

Ralegh's Muster-Roll, 1587

STATE PAPERS—IRELAND, 1587.

BUNDLE 129. NO. 77.

Sr Walter Rawleigh knight his musteroll taken before Sr Thomas Norys, xi May 1587.

Andrewe Clothurst Capten
Thoms Colthurst lyfeten'nt
Rob't Mawley
George longe
Godfrey bricklaid
John Warren
Geoffrey tottell
Thoms Dowdall
Edmond Wicklow
Ambrose Wyld
fferdoro m^c Shey
Chachire m^c donogh
John fitz gerrott

Q   Phillip

Phillip thickpeny
Will'm love
Robert Pyndie
John Lee
Nicholas Lawrence
Thom's Sewell
Thoms blacklett

VI

Lord Burghley's Notes of Ralegh's Opinions as to the Forces to be kept in Munster

STATE PAPERS—IRELAND, 1582, OCTOBER.

BUNDLE 96. NOS. 30, 31.

The opinio' of Mr. Rawley vppo' motio's made to hym for ye meanes of subdvy'g ye rebellio' in Monster.

first he thynketh that the Q. Ma^y forces alone w'out a' excessyve chardg by a' army y^t may s'rve to laye garriso's in every cou'trye, will not subdew ye rebell. for he shall be so releved in every contrye, where the e'glish souldiors ca'not follow hym, as by flyi'g fro' co'ntry to co'ntry he will hold vp his head a long tyme.

Therfor he thynketh it nedefull to have ye help and concurre'cy of dyvers lords of particular co'ntryes to ioyne in this servyce and herin he sayth, ther ar man'y such at this tyme y^t adhere to ye Erle of Desmo'd, which hertofor was good sub-

Q 2   iects

iects and s'rved ageynst the Erle, and so'e of them
being evill vsed by ye English soldiors, and havy'g
an opinio' y^t in the end, her Ma^ty will both pardo'
and restore the Erle as hertofor he hath bene, they
do ye rather follow hym for feare, to be hereaft^r
played by hy', if now they should not follow hy'
And therfor if man'y of them war p^ivatly delt
w^tall to retorn to ye s^rvice of hir Ma^ty, and to be
pmitted to possess ther ow' co'ntryes getly, and war
well pswaded that the Erle shuld never be restored,
they wold be brought to s'rve hir Ma^ty, and i'peach
ye rebell fro' entry into ther co'ntryes and so hir
Ma^ty Garriso's might to more purpooss both defend
other co'ntryes worth defence and also ye more
savely purseu ye Rebell.

And to explane this generall opinio' in a pticular
sort.

It is thovght good y^t these psons hereafter named
might be revocked by pardo' to hir Ma^ys s'rvice,
wherby ye Erle shall be left very weak, and shall
have almost no place to co'tynew in.

The first is ye Lord Fitzmoryce, baro' of Lex-
naw who in all former tymes hath hated ye Erle
of Desmo'd and suffred gret damag's by w^t-
standy'g of him and hath allweis sovght to be
defended agay'st the Erle by ye Q. Ma^ty. this ma'
being reclaymid, a small to of hir Ma^ty forces

cov'tena'cy'g

cov'tena'cy'g hym, shall kepe ye Erle out of Kyrry, or els shall so cross hym if he become thyth' as he shall not be hable to tarry long there.

The second is to have Don'ogh McCormock y^t was com'itted p'soner to Cork for p'tendy'g right to ye Co'ntry called Dowallay, to be also by pardo' revocqued to hir Ma^tys S'vice, and to be restored to his own Co'ntry, wherto he hath right, and at this tyme, a child, pr'soner therto, whose father slew Don'oghs father being ye lawfull possessor of ye Co'ntry. this ma' hath hertofore s'rved also agey'st the rebell, and being com'itted to pr'son, after he escaped, he avowed only to recov' his own co'trey, and not to s'rve agey'st any e'glishma'.

Condon is of least force & hathe bin p'doned often.

The third pso' tobe recovered, is patryck Co'do' lord of ye Condo's co'ntreye and s'rveth the Erle at this tyme but for feare of his restitutio', for his co'ntreye is subiect allweise to ye spoyle of ye Erle.

the white knighte was never yet ioyned wth the Earle but stands vppon his kepinge.

The 4th pso' is ye whyt knyght, on also y^t hath s'rved the Qu. and mete to be draw' fro' ye Erle.

All wch psons ar to be recovered cheifly by the Erle of Ormo'd or by suche as one as the countrey hathe good likinge vnto.

If these 4 may be recovered fro' ye Erle they and the rest y^t ar sownd subiects as all y^e

Mackartyes,

Mackartyes, ye more, reagh, ye lord Roche, power, and now ye vico't barryes, w^t the Q. forces placed as hereaft^r ar named, shall be hable to subdew ye Erle and all ye rest of his followers, w^t will not be man'y to co'tynew.

It'm. these 4 pso's being recovered fro' ye Erle may be also induced to surre'der ther Co'ntreyes to hir Ma^ty, and to receive them by gra't from hir Ma^ty, yeldy'g a certen rent, to be discharged of Cess to souldiors.

     The opinio' for placy'g of ye Garriso's.

At Killmallock	horsem.	l	
	footeme'	ij^c	
at Mallo vppo' ye brode water	horss'	xx	
	footeme'	j^c	ij^cxx.
In tipperary	horssme'	j^c	

     I think to p'forme the service thereby ther shall need thes companies,

       In Killmallocke 200 foot' & 50 horse.

       At Malo or ther aboute as manye.

       In the border of Tiberary 100 horse the bande of Carbery to defend the west p't therof & serve vppon the macswynes wch amountethe vnto 500 footmen & 200 horse beside wardes wch forces may be continewed for a short tyme vntill the lords above named be drawen from the Earle, then cashed & supply other bandes.

                                     In

In Carberry footemen   j^e

In ye Wards of		
Asskettyn . .	12	
ly'merick . .	6	
Castell many .	12	
ye Glandy (?) .	8	r^{o}x
Di'gle . . .	32	
lovghyrr (?) .	4	
Yowghall . .	20	
Do'garva' . .	16	

Totall horssme' . j^{e}lxx
footme' . iiij^e vj^{e}lxxxx
Wards . j^{o}x

Of the 20 at Asketon & the 10 at Limbrick ther may be taken away 10 and added to the 20 of the dingle levinge at Limbrick Castle 6, & at Asketon 14, and 30 at Dingle, it may be inquired whether they of the Dingle will not vndertake to keepe some place of them sealves wthout a warde as I have heard they will.

It is also necessary that all y^e soldiors be so p'vyded o^r in ther paye as they lyve not vppo' y$^.$ Cess of y^e Contry, for if they shall, y^e disorder ca' not be avoyded, but the people will be so opposed, as they will rather adhere to y^e rebells, than to suffer y^e pilladg of y^e soldior. The Victualls, munic'on, & tresor for Mounstre should be sent to Corke or Lymbricke & not had from Debelin.

It'm. ye lords of ye severall co'ntryes may be induced, to contribut to hir Ma^{ty} sondry soo's of mon'y in reco'pe'ce of ye burthe' of Cess wherin.

now

now at yᵉ begy'nyng so'e moderatio' wold be vsed, because yᵉ co'ntryes ar gretly wasted but aftʳ or.

The Erle of Desmo'd.

In Inskelly.   The Seneshall.

in Arlogh.   Garrett fitz Thomas of yᵉ Geraldy's.

        yᵉ principall sept of yᵉ Browns   blyck brow', son to Thomas brow' yᵗ was slayn. Jho' brow' was slayn whose dorghtʳ Appsley marryed.

in Con'elogh.   Nich. fitzwᵐˢ yᵉ recevor kylled by estoft he was M'shall   killed by Brya' Mᶜ Don'ell Myrryck yᵉ Erle of Capt. of ye Erles kernlygh Ormo'd.

        Mᶜ Cann in Co'nelogh

        Mʳ Thomas of yᵉ pallace killed by yᵉ whyt knight with xxiiij mo. by order of yᵉ Erle of Ormo'd.

        Mʳ Mack Thomas he lyveth.

in Ker'y betwixt Aden and Askety.

        Pursell so'n of p'sell of Ballyholla' vppon yᵉ Ryver of Adar yᵗ was chac.' of lym'eryck.

    The Whyt Knight.   Edmu'd fitz Gibbon als' Edmu'd Mᶜ Rvddery so' to Gibbo's yᵗ was attaynted.

VII

Sir Walter Ralegh's Lease of Cuil-na-clocfionna ("the Nook of the White Stone") *

THIS INDENTURE made the one and twentieth day of July in the thirtith yeare of the raign of our Soveraign Ladie Elizabeth by the grace of God of England, Fraunce and Ireland, Queene, Defendor of the faith &c. Between the honorable Sir Walter Ralegh, Knight, Warden of her Majesties Stanneries in the counties of Devon and Cornewall and one of the principall undertakers with her Majestie for the repeoplinge and inhabitinge the attainted and escheated lands in the counties of Corke and Waterfourd in the Province of Munster in her highnes Realme of Ireland of thone partie, And John Clever of London, gentleman of thother

---

* From the original preserved at Ralegh's house. His signature and seal were cut off and exhibited in England some years ago, and then returned to Youghal. The precis on the back, "21 July, 1588. Cuolycloghsy Fynnay leased for a 100 yeares, commencing the 30th yeare Elizæ reginæ," is in his handwriting.

partie,

partie, Witnesseth that the said Sir Walter Ralegh
for divers good causes and reasonable considerations him hereunto especially movinge, Hath
demised, graunted, betaken and to farme letten,
and by these presents doth demise, graunte, betake
and to farme lett unto the said John Clever, all that
ploughland commonly called or knowen by the
name of Coultie Closinia sett and beinge within the
Barrony Inchequyn Ralegh in the countie of Corke
aforesaid, with foure hundred acres of arrable land
and ferme, woods, hereunto belonginge, and if
there be not foure hundered acres of arrable land
and farme within the said plough land of Coultie
Closynia aforesaid.   Then the said Sir Walter
Ralegh willeth and graunteth, and by these
presents doth demise and graunt unto the said
John Clever, that there shall be taken out of the
lands of Polla-more, or out of the lands next
adjoyninge unto the aforesaid Coultie Closynia as
much as together with the farme woods, shall make
upp the just number of foure hundred acres of
arrable land, the same to be measured by the
Standard measure of Winchester, within the Realme
of England.   Together with all, and hill, mountain
of woods, underwoods, waters, weares, Rivers,
poulls, fords, marshes, moors, boggs, mountains,
barren heaths, wast grounds, comons, foullinge,

fishinge,

fishinge, hawkinge, huntinge, and all other profits, comodities and advantages whatsoever, to the same premises belonging, or in any wise apperteyning. Except and allwayes reserved out of thes present demise and graunte unto the said Sir Walter Ralegh his heires and assignes the Royalties of the same premises and all wreackes of the sea, that shall happen within the same premisses, To have and to hold all and singular the same demised premisses and every parcell thereof with the appurtenances (except before excepted) unto the said John Clever, his executors and assignes, from the feast of Sainct Michaell the Archangell next ensuing the date hereof unto the end and tearme of one hundred years from thence next ensuinge and fully to be compleat and ended. Yielding and Payinge therefore yearely, duringe three of the said yeares, (viz.) from the end of the year of our Lord God, which shall be one Thowsand five hundred foure score and nyne, from and after the decease of the Ladie Cattelyn old Countesse dowager of Desmound, widdowe, untill the end of the yeare of our Lord God, which shall be, 1593, unto the said Sir Walter Ralegh, his heires or assignes, five pounds of good and lawful money of England, at two feasts or tearmes of the year, that is to say, at the feasts of the Aununciation of our

Ladie

Ladie S^t. Mary, the Virgine and S^t. Michæl The Archangell, by even portions, and also fower capons or hennes, at the feasts of Easter and Christmas, if they be demanded, and also yeldinge and payinge therefore yearly to the said Sir Walter Ralegh his heires or assignes during the residue of the said terme, beginning from and after the decease of the said Countesse, and after the end of the said yeare of our Lord God, which shall be 1593, the yearly rent of Tenne pounds of lawful money of England, at the said two feasts, which of them shall first happen after the death of the said Countess and after the end of the said year, 1593, the first payment thereof shall begyne and also fower capons or hennes, at the feasts of Easter and Christmas, if they be demanded, And if it shall happen, either the said yearly rents of five pounds or tenne pounds to be behind and unpaid, in part or in all, after any of the said feasts, in which the same ought to be paid, by the space of one whole year, being lawfully demanded, and no sufficient distresse in or upon the same premises may or can be found. That then and from thencefourth, this present lease, demise and graunte and every article and sentence therein conteyned shall be utterly void and of none effect, Any thinge herein conteyned to the contrary notwithstanding, And

the

the said John Clever for himself his executors, Administrators and Assignes covenenteth and graunteth, to and with the said Sir Walter Ralegh his heires and assignes by these presents, to find from tyme to tyme, after the decease of the said Countesse and after the end of the said year 1593 a sufficient light horse with man and furniture, to the said Sir Walter Ralegh, his heires and assignes in the affairs of the Croune of Ireland, And also shall and will, at his and their oune proper costs and charge, erect, build upp and fynishe, in and by all things one mansion or dwelling house in and upon the same premises, at or before the feast of S^t. Michæl, which shall be 1593. And shall also before the same feast, at his and their proper costs and charges &c., likewise enclose with hedge, ditche and quicke sett, one hundred acres, and keep the same in good and sufficient reparation and fencinge. And the same so well and sufficiently repared and amended, in the end of the said tearme or other evacuation of this present demise, shall leave and yeld upp unto the said Sir Walter Ralegh, his heires or assignes for every acre of bogg, mountaine or barren heath, that is or shall be converted to good ground, one penny sterlinge, if it shall so sale out, that the Queenes Majestie, her heires or successors shall

have

have or demand of the said Sir Walter Ralegh
his heires or assignes for every acre of the same
land one farthinge or half penny. And also shall
leave at every fall of any of the woods of the same
premises, Twenty and five stands in every acre,
according to the custom of England.

And the said Sir Walter Ralegh for himself and
his heires, executors and assignes, doth covenant,
promise and grant to and with the said John
Clever, his executors and assignes, by theis
presents, that he the said John Clever, his
executors and assignes, for the several yearly
rents before in theis presents reserved, and under
the covenants, graunts, articles and agreements
herein conteyned, which on his or their parts are
and ought to be observed and kept, shall or may
by virtue hereof peaceablie and quietly have, hold,
occupie, possess and enjoy the same demised
premises and every parcell thereof, with the
appurtenances, (except before excepted) without
any lawful lett, troble, deniall, or interruption of
the said Sir Walter Ralegh his heires or assignes,
discharged or otherwise sufficiently saved or kept
harmless, as well of and from all and all manner
of former bargaynes, sales, guifts, grants, leases,
trobles, chardges, and incombrances whatsoever,
As also of all bond services, Irishe customes

arrerages

arrerages of rents and other endempnities whatsoever had, made or done, or caused to be done
by the said Sir Walter Ralegh, his heires or
assignes, or by any other person or persons,
whatsoever claymynge from, by, or under him,
them or any of them, during the foresaid terme.
In Witnes whereof the said parties to these
present Indentures interchaungablie have put
their hands and seals.

```
┌──────────────┐   ┌──────────────┐
│  Sir W. R.'s │   │              │
│     Seal     │   │  W. Ralegh   │
│              │   │              │
└──────────────┘   └──────────────┘
```

Yeoven the day and yeare first above
written   ' .   Mem. that this word
(Closynia) amended in three   .
Indenture as aforesaid was done with the
assents   , parties before thensealinge
hereof.   Teste me Nichols   .   .

Recognitum coram me Laur. Husc' uno Magistrorum
                                        cancellarii
dictæ dominæ reginæ, secundo die Augusti, anno regni
                                        sui supradicto.

Endorsed : " *Sigillatum et deliberatum in presentiâ mei
        Henrici Donoghty, scriba.*"

VIII

Royal Warrant, under the Sign Manual and Signet *

By the Queen.

For the Countesse of Desmond, to the Lord Deputy.

ELIZABETH. R.

Right trusty and welbeloved, we greete you well. Whereas the Countesse of Desmond hath bene an humble suitor unto us, to releve her poore estate and miserye, wherunto she is brought by her late husband's rebellion against us. We having compassion of her, are pleased of our gracious princely favor, for her releefe to bestowe upon her, a yeerly pencion of twoo hundred pounds sterling, to be quarterly paid unto her or her assignes, out of our Exchequer, of that our Relm, during our pleasure, And therfore we will and commaund you to cause a patent to be made from us, and passed under our greate Seale, of that our Relm of Ireland, of the said

* From the original preserved at Ralegh's house.

annuity

annuity of 11 hundred pounds by yeere, to be paid quarterly as aforesaid from the feast of the Annunciation of our Lady 1587, to the said Countess, by the hands of our Tresorer at warres there for the tyme being, eyther of such monny as comith to his hands of our Revenue there, or of such treasure as shall be from time to tyme assigned from our hands to him for that our Relm, and the same to be charged in the accompt, for that our Relm. Willing you furder to have that care, and to take such order for the sure payment of the abovesayd yearly pencion there, to the said Countess and her assignes, that she may not fayle thereof, at the termes the same shall be due, and that she may have no just cause to complayin, for want of payment of the same. And these our letter, notwitstanding any want of woords, that might be here omitted, and were required to be inserted for this purpose, which nevertheless, We declare are inserted, or any other cause or matter whatsoever, shall be unto you our deputy now being, or to any other deputie or Governor of that Relm that shall be for the tyme, and to the Tresurer at warre, their for the tyme being, and to any other our officers, ministers to whom it may in this case appertayn, shall be sufficient warrant and discharge in this behalfe. Gyven under our Signett at our Mannor

R   of

of S^t. James's, the second of October 1588, in the Thirtith yeare of our Rayne."

" To our right trusty and welbeloved Sir William Fitzwillms, Knight, deputy of our Relm of Ireland, and to any deputy or other head Gouvernor there, that hereafter shall be, and to our Chauncelor there now being, and Chauncelor or Keeper of our great-Seale of Ireland hereafter to be. And to the Tresurer at Warre that now is, and that hereafter shall be of that our Relm, and to any other our officers or ministers there, to whom it doth or shall apparteyin."

Endorsed :
" *Inrolled on the Patent Roll of Ireland, in the thirty second year of the reign of our Queen Elizabeth.*" (Seal beneath.)

IX

Ralegh and Florence McCarthy in the Tower together*

The demaundes of Sr George Haruie Knight Lieveten'nte of the Tower of London for the dietts and charges of Prisoners in his custodie for one whole Quarter of a yeare vizt :—from the feast of St: Michaell tharkangell 1603 vntill the feast of the Natiuitie and Birth of Christ next followinge, As hereafter is declared.

After charges for the late Lo: Cobham and the late Lo: Gray of Wilton,

Sr Walter Raleigh knight.	Item for the diett and charges of Sr Walter Raleigh knight for himsealf and two s^{r}nnts from the xvjth of December, being then sentt from Winchester, to the Tower againe, for one weeke and a halfe ended the xxvth of December att iiij^l the weeke—	vj^l

Then follow the charges for Bartholomewe Brookesby Esquio^r, Anthony Copley Esquior, Sr Griffin Marckham knight, Lawrence Kennthe Esquior, Patrick Ruthen, William Watson, Preist, William Clark Preist, Nicholas Kendall, Gentleman.

* The original in the State Paper Office, London.

fflorence Ma^cartie	Item, for the diett and charges of fflorence McCharthie ffrom the xxixth of September 1603 vntill the xxvth of Decemb'r next following being xij weekes and half at liij^s iiij^d the weeke———	xxxiiij^l vj^s viij^d	xx^l iiij^s xj^s
	Item, more for Apparrell and other Necessaries bowght for him this Quarter———	xliiij^s iiij^d	
Jeames Ma^cThomas	Item, for the diett and Charges of Jeames Ma^cThomas in the ffleete from the ixth daye of Maye 1603 vnto the xth daye of August being xiij weekes for himsealf and A s'nnte at xl^s the weeke———	xxvj^l	lxxij^l j^s iiij^d
	Item, for the diett and Charges of Jeames Ma^cThomas the Tituler Erle of Desmond from the xxixth of September 1603 vntill the xxvth of Decemb'r next ffollowinge being xij weekes and halfe att iij^l the weeke———	xxxvij^l x^s	
	Item, for Apparrell and Necessaries bowght for him this Quarter———	vij^l xj^s iiij^d	

Then follow the charges for Roger Gwynn, Preist, the Phisition, the Apothecarie, the Barbour.

Sum of Allowauces for Prisoners dietts and charges, ffor the Phisition, Appothecarie and Barbour this Quarter———	ccccxlj^l xvij^s ij^d

T. Ellesmere, Canc.'   T. Buckhurst.

Suffolke.   Ro. Cecyll.   E. Wotton.

L. Stanhope,

G. Haruy, locut' Turr'.

X

Ralegh and the Eighteenth Earl of Desmond in the Tower *

The demaunds of Sr George Heruye Knight Leiueten'nte of the Tower of London for the Dietts and other Charges of Prisoners in his Custodie, for one whole Quarter of a yeere vizt from the ffeast of the Natiuitie and birth of Christ 1604 vntill the ffeast of the Annunc'ac'on of our Lady next following, as heereafter is declared.

The late Lord Cobham.	Imprimis for the diett and charges of the late Lord Cobham and his three Seruaunts from Xpmas 1604 vnto the Annuc'ac'on of our Lady next ffollowing 1605 being Thirtene weeks att viij*l* the weeke———	ciiij*l*
The late Lord Gray.	Item, for the diett and Charges of the Late Lord Gray for himself and three Ser'nnts from xpmas: 1604 vntill our Lady daye 1605 next ffollowing being Thirteene weeks att viij*l* a weeke	ciiij*l*

---

* The original is in the State Paper Office, London.

Item,

Sir Walter Raleigh Kn^t.	Item, for the diett and Charges of Sr Walter Raleigh Knight for himself and three Seruants from xpmas 1604 vntill our Lady daye next ffollowing 1605 being Thirteene weekes at v^l a weeke—	lxv^l	
James Mc Thomas.	Item for the diett and charges of James McThomas Tituler Erle of Dessmond, from xpmas: 1604 vntill our Lady daye 1605 next ffollowing being Thirteene weeks at iij^l a weeke———	xxxix^l	xlviij^l ij^d
	Item more for Apparell and necessaries bowght for him this Quarter———	iiij^l ij^d	
	Item, more for his washing this Quarter v^s in toto———	v^s	

Then follow the charges for Patrick Ruthen, Thomas Pound, Brian Bridger, Doctor Sharpp, and Thomas Bywater.

The Phisition.	Item, to Doctor Ellwin phisition for visiting the sick prisoners this Quarter———	v^l
The Appothecarie.	Item, to Roger Gwinn apothecarie for Phisick ministred to the Prisoners this Quarter, his bill——	viij^l xviij^s
The Barbour.	Item, to Edward Porter, barbour for trymming the Prisoners this Quarter———	xlv^s

Sum'a. of allowancs for Prisoners dietts and charges for the Phisition, Apothecarie and Barbour this Quarter——	iiij^c xlj^l xiiij^s viij^d

T. Dorset.   Lenox.   E. Worcester.   Cumberland.

Cranborne.   E. Wotton.   L. Stanhope.

G. Heruye Locut. Turr.

INDEX

INDEX

regal state and conciliatory policy, 127-8 ; toleration to
Catholics and interview with Tyrone, 129 ; censured by
the Queen, and names Ralegh as her adviser, 130 ; calls
Ralegh a fox, 131, 147

S

LONDON:
PRINTED BY WILLIAM CLOWES AND SONS, LIMITED,
STAMFORD STREET AND CHARING CROSS.